James Franklin Fitts

A Sharp Night's Work

A powerful detective story

James Franklin Fitts

A Sharp Night's Work
A powerful detective story

ISBN/EAN: 9783337028381

Printed in Europe, USA, Canada, Australia, Japan

Cover: Foto ©Andreas Hilbeck / pixelio.de

More available books at **www.hansebooks.com**

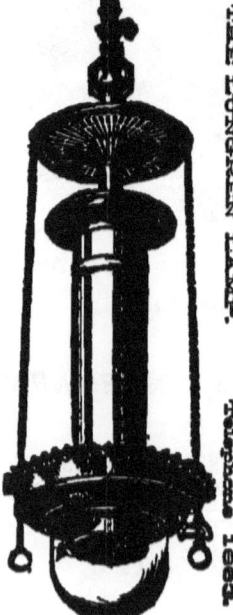

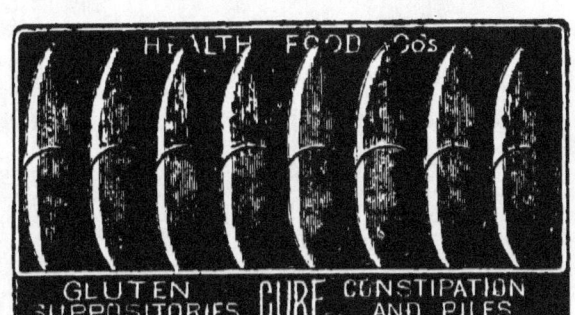

A LEAP FOR LIFE.—Page 36.

A SHARP NIGHT'S WORK

A POWERFUL DETECTIVE STORY

BY

JAMES FRANKLIN FITTS

—

CHICAGO
LAIRD & LEE PUBLISHERS
CLARK AND ADAMS STREETS

CONTENTS.

Chapter.		Page
I.	The Starting Point	9
II.	Startling News	14
III.	To the Rescue!	20
IV.	On the Track	26
V.	A Desperate Expedient	32
VI.	No Such Word as Fail	38
VII.	The Unexpected Happens	43
VIII.	The Last Rally	49
IX.	The Evil Eye	53
X.	The Course of True Love	56
XI.	The Trail of the Serpent	62
XII.	The Detective Appears	69
XIII.	The Silent Witness	75
XIV.	The Detective at Work	81
XV.	Shadowed by Night	84
XVI.	The Woman in the Case	87
XVII.	Under the Spell	93
XVIII.	Perverse Fates	97
XIX.	The Telegram	100
XX.	After the Marriage	104
XXI.	An Escape	109
XXII.	In Swift Pursuit	112
XXIII.	Too Late!	116
XXIV.	Baffled!	119
XXV.	Light Breaks	125
XXVI.	In Darkness and Distress	131
XXVII.	Refuge and Discovery	135
XXVIII.	Retribution and Reunion	138
XXIX.	Sunshine Through the Clouds	144
XXX.	A Horror of the Night	149
XXXI.	The Voice of Death	154
XXXII.	The Detective's New Revelation	158
XXXIII.	Recompense	165
XXXIV.	Last Scene of All	168

A SHARP NIGHT'S WORK

CHAPTER I.

THE STARTING POINT.

TUESDAY, September 18th, 1877, at 2:33 p. m., the Western accommodation was precisely on time at Granby Station. One passenger only alighted there; and as the train departed without gaining any travelers at this point, the man was left standing alone in the middle of the platform fronting the little station. Not another human creature was at the moment in sight. The weather was unusually hot for the time, and a bright sun glared down upon the traveler. As his eye glanced all about him, taking in his surroundings, he looked unmistakably weary. He had no baggage, not even a hand-satchel. He was of medium height, spare of form and face, with iron-gray hair, prominent features, face slightly wrinkled, and such blue eyes as he who once saw would turn to look at again. They were of that cold, expressionless hue, which, accompanying a thin-lipped mouth and Roman nose, give the observer no kind of index to the character of the man, or even to his present thoughts. His form was erect, spite of the fact that his years were nearer sixty than fifty. As to his real character there need be no concealment here. He was a veteran detective, grown old and gray in the skilled business of unearthing great crimes and bringing to justice great criminals against wealthy corporations at the West; and although he had lately retired from this exciting and lucrative pursuit, and had come East on an errand, the nature of which will in due time be disclosed, he had undertaken the journey of this day, not only because his heart was in its object, but because his detective ability was urgently demanded to insure its success.

The ticket agent within slammed down the window of his office, and walked lazily out into the hot sunshine. The traveler accosted him:

" How far is it to Granby village? "

" Nine miles."

" Is there no conveyance? "

The agent laughed.

"Sometimes there is; sometimes not. It depends."

" Is there one to-day? " the other impatiently asked.

" By present appearances, I should say not. This seems to be one of Simple Simon's off-days. Fact is," he continued, in a half-apologetic tone, " it ain't more'n once a week that anybody gets on or off here. When there's anybody coming over from the village who'll pay Simple Simon, as we call him, a quarter to bring him, he'll hitch up his old sorrel and come. Other times, when he feels like ramblin' over to see if there's somebody stopped off, he comes; but he ain't to be depended on."

Possessed of so much of the unpromising situation, the traveler snapped his fingers briskly, and sent out questions and remarks as sharply as needle points.

" Where can I hire a conveyance to go over to the village?"

" You can't hire one."

" What—has nobody here got a horse and buggy?"

" Nobody but me; and I don't hire mine."

" What might your horse and buggy be worth?"

The pride of the country ticket agent was touched; this man wanted to talk with him about his horse, the darling of his heart!

" Well, sir," he said, " he's a *good* animal. He can make a mile in four minutes."

" Indeed!" said the traveler, humoring him.

" Fact! And that buggy was new only three years ago."

" I asked you what they are worth?"

" Dunno as I want to sell; but the horse ain't worth a cent less than a hundred an' fifty; and the buggy's worth a hundred more."

" See here," and the traveler spoke rapidly and with decision: " I've got to go to Granby, and get back here in time for the west-bound night express. What's its time?"

" Six twenty-seven."

" I say I *must* go over now, and return here in time for that train. I would give you twenty dollars for the use of your rig; yet, as the day is very sultry, and time presses me, I cannot promise to spare horseflesh. You say the establishment is worth two hundred and fifty dollars; I'll buy it of you and give you fifty dollars over. If you choose to take it back to-night at a fair valuation, well and good; if not, I shall not complain. Here!"

The speaker drew a plethoric wallet from his pocket, extracted from its contents three one hundred dollar bills, and offered them to the agent. The latter mechanically took the money, but remonstrated with amazement.

" It's a dreadful fair offer; but you haven't seen the horse, nor——"

" The bargain is closed, sir ! " interrupted the traveler, peremptorily. We are wasting valuable time; fly around lively, now; I must be on the road."

The ticket agent hurried away to his barn, near at hand, thinking that his luck was wonderful that afternoon, and wishing he might know what lunatic it was that had just given him three hundred dollars for property that would have been dear at two hundred, and that without seeing it. But the new rustling bank notes in his hand hastened his movements, and in ten minutes horse and buggy were ready at the rear of the

station. Without another word as to the arrangement
he had made for the return of the property, the traveler climed into the vehicle, and, waiting only to get
directions as to the road, he laid on the whip at the
start, and was off like a shot.

The astonished agent watched him as he disappeared
in a cloud of dust, above which he could see the wav-
ing whiplash. He had not so much as learned the
man's name!

"Escaped from some mad-house, sure!" was his
comment. "He'll break his neck long before he gets
to the village."

It was just three o'clock when our traveler left the
Granby Station. The animal that he drove might
have been as good as recommended, ordinarily; upon
such a day and such a dusty road, he certainly was not.
His driver did not spare him. Never once in that long
nine-mile stretch was the poor beast suffered to walk
more than a minute at a time. The whip often
descended on his dusty, sweaty flanks, and his long-
reaching trot was not suffered to lag.

"I pity you, poor beast!" the old detective once
murmured, as he noticed the evident distress of the
animal. "Thousands upon thousands of miles have I
driven over the rough Western highways, and ever
have been merciful to the horse; but this is not the
time to think of such things." And the whip cracked
again.

In several houses on the long, straggling street of
Granby village the clocks were striking four as the
panting, sweating horse, with hanging head and quivering flank, stopped before the inn. The landlord
came out in his shirt-sleeves; two or three loungers on
the bench before the house roused themselves sufficiently to stare at the new comer, and wonder who he
was, any way.

The detective jumped out.

"Landlord," he said, "look sharp here!—listen.

"Do you see this?" and he thrust a ten-dollar note into his hand. " That will pay you well for all you can do for me. I want your time, *your wits*, and your best service, quickly given. Have that horse taken out, thoroughly rubbed down, watered in twenty minutes—not before—fed, and then harnessed, ready to be put in the shafts in a minute. See to this, and then come back.

Stimulated by the great liberality just shown, the landlord succeeded in infusing vitality enough into a couple of the loungers to get these directions obeyed.

" Now, then, listen to me," said the detective, leading the landlord off to the end of the platform, out of hearing. " I'm looking for a man; he is here in this village, somewhere. His name is Ernest Mulford. Do you know him?"

" Hain't no such man here," was the prompt reply.

" Are you sure?"

" Sartin sure. There's a matter of less'n three hundred people in Granby, and I know 'em all—every sinner of 'em. Nobody o' that name here, I tell you."

" The *name* don't count for much ; it is the *man* I want. Nothing is put off and on as easily as a name. Are there any strangers in the village?"

" Nary one."

The detective's face clouded.

" But since July, say only two months back. Just think, now, and see if you can't remember that strangers, new people, have come in here within that time, and stayed."

The landlord rubbed the stubble on his chin thoughtfully, and said, slowly:

" Why—ye-e-s; I guess there has been one or two. What sorter man you lookin' for?"

" I have never seen him ; but he is described to me by many people, who have seen him, as five feet eleven in height; slim and active; brown eyes and hair; ruddy face; about twenty-six years old. Now, what do you say?"

The landlord heard, and a remarkable change came over his stolid countenance. A broad ray of intelligence lighted it. He significantly pointed backward with his thumb over his shoulder.

"You're pretty good on describin', stranger," he said, "you've just exactly hit off a young fellow that came here 'long the middle or last of July, an' hain't done nothing since but write letters and never get any; take long walks all by himself; watch at the postoffice for letters that never come, and make a fool of himself gen'r'ly. He's been stayin' here with me, and he's lyin' on that bench there this minute. He goes by the name of Martin Sammons.

The detective turned abruptly, and, with his hands behind his back, walked the length of the platform in front of the inn. At the further end he turned and walked back. Each time he passed a little nearer to the lounger on the bench, and each time upon passing he shot a swift glance that way. Finally he halted and stood still, directly before him. The lounger opened his èyes, and drowsily took in the appearance of the stranger. He closed them again, when the detective's voice, low as it was, broke like a thunder-clap on his dozing senses:

"Well, Ernest Mulford, how do you find yourself?"

CHAPTER II.

STARTLING NEWS.

THE young man sprang to his feet and looked wildly at the detective. He was thoroughly roused and alarmed, and the blood fled from his cheek. He stood speechless, confronting the man who had addressed him. The latter stood carelessly, with his hands behind his back, returning the young man's gaze with a

quiet look. His face was absolutely without expression.

" Well! " he said.

" My name is not Ernest Mulford," the other protested.

" Oh yes, it is. Don't deny it. I know you, sir! "

The young man heard the quiet, determined tone,
and saw the resolute eyes that steadily regarded him.
A common expression best describes the effect produced upon him. He *weakened*. Sinking down upon
the bench again, he said, with a sigh:

" Let it be so, then. I don't care. Arrest me, if
you will. Only, mind, I don't admit any wrong-
doing! I'm innocent of crime, I say! "

" This is no place to talk such things over," replied
the detective. " Come inside with me. I want you to
go with me to the station; but I've something to say to
you first. "

He led the way into the shabby little parlor of the
inn, the other doggedly following him. The detective
locked the doors.

" You admit, then, that you are Ernest Mulford? "

" Yes. What of it? "

" You shall hear. I am Elias Lear, late chief of detectives for several great Western railroads. Perhaps
you have heard of me. "

" Yes; but I don't care. If you are going to arrest
me.——"

" I am not going to arrest you," said Mr. Lear,
quietly. " When you said out there, a moment since,
that you had not committed any crime, you told the
truth. But you have acted foolishly, and without judgment. "

Mulford began to speak, but Mr. Lear silenced him
with a motion of his hand, and went on.

" It is barely eight weeks ago since you left the village of Bardwell, secretly and at night. Two motives
prompted you. The girl you loved had rejected your

suit, as you thought, and your heart was filled with bitterness. Just at that time your employer peremptorily dismissed you without giving any true reason for so doing. These two misfortunes so wrought upon you that you hastily and unwisely determined to fly from the place where you had been honored and respected for years. Is this true?"

Ernest Mulford sat with folded arms, his eyes bent upon the floor, silent under this recital.

"Since you left," pursued Lear, "gossip and rumor have been busy with your name. It has been reported, and it is generally believed, that you were discovered by your employer in thefts from his safe; that he accused you, and that, on your confession, he agreed not to prosecute you provided you would leave town at once. This story, I may say, is believed by nine-tenths of the people of that village."

"But it is false," was the sullen reply. "I don't know that it is any of your business, but since you will talk about it, I will say that you have found out one good reason for my leaving Bardwell. Right off, after that, when Mr. Mayhew discharged me without fair explanation, I did feel upset, and I left without a word to anybody. You say it was unwise; I don't know nor care. I have done with that town and its people; they will never see me again."

"You will reconsider that determination, Mr. Mulford, within the next fifteen minutes. Did it never occur to you that there was some connection between your dismissal by that lady and your dismissal by Mr. Mayhew?"

Mulford started to his feet.

"Sit down again, sir; be quiet; let us talk. Have you heard anything from Bardwell since you left there?"

"No; not a word."

"Have you written?"

Mulford hesitated. Mr. Lear took his hand, and

addressed him in a tone of frankness and cordiality such as he had not before used.

"Mr. Mulford, we must have an understanding at once. I want you to return to Bardwell with me; but it will not be by compulsion. I have come here as your friend; some day you shall know what it was that made me labor earnestly for you; it is too long a story to tell now. Believe me, I want to help you to right yourself and to prevent the consummation of the most outrageous villainy against you and another. Will you trust me?"

The honest manliness of the words and of the face at that moment prevailed over the young man's doubts and bewilderment. He silently returned the pressure of the hand that had taken his.

"Thank you; you do well to trust me. Now tell me why you are still lingering here if you have heard nothing from Bardwell since you left there?"

"Because it is only a few hours' journey from there, I suppose. Because," and his tone grew bitter, "because, like many another fool before me, I can't take a woman's 'No,' and end it. Twenty times I have resolved to go to New York and enlist in the regulars, or ship before the mast; once I got as far as Granby Station on my way—and I couldn't go. Idiot that I am, I can't give her up."

The pent-up feelings of the distressed lover almost prevailed against his manhood. He lowered his head, and the quick ear of the other heard a stifled sob.

"And you have written to her?"

"Yes; and to others. But nothing has come back to me?"

"I suppose you did not think," drily remarked Lear, "of Mr. Weston Mayhew's commission as postmaster at Bardwell?"

Mulford looked up. Very slowly the sinister meaning of the detective's words came to him. Then,

A Sharp Night's Work 2

as if moved by an electric shock, he bounded to his
feet.

"Great heaven, sir!" he cried, "you don't mean
that that man——"   '

"Weston Mayhew," interrupted Mr. Lear, "is
capable of anything to secure his coveted ends. What
he has done and what he proposes to do, you need not
trust my word for; here it is in black and white. Look!
read! and then say if you are not only willing but
anxious to go back with me."

He drew from an inner pocket a large, square, stiff
envelope. It seemed filled with inclosures. First, he
took from it a piece of Bristol board, upon one side of
which were, neatly joined together and pasted, the torn
and minute fragments of a letter. The envelope, bear-
ing the Granby postmark, restored in the same way,
was pasted upon the other side of the board. Save
one small fragment the letter was complete, and easily
legible.

"That is your writing, I presume," said Lear.

"One of my letters to *her!*" gasped Mulford.
"Where did you get it?"

"*She* never saw it ; you ought to be able to conjecture, after what I have told you, the reason why. Well,
we must hasten ; we have but a few minutes more to
spend over these things. Look over these quickly,"
and he took more inclosures from the envelope. There
were five of them. With much labor and skill the torn
and scattered fragments had been collected and
restored.

"These are all that I wrote to her," said Mulford
through his teeth.

Mr. Lear tapped the envelope. "Here are also three
letters that you mailed here to friends at Bardwell.
Not one of them was delivered to its address."

"In the name of all that is wonderful, sir, how did
you get them and put them together this way?"

"No matter now. I can't spend time to tell you.

Such work is only a bagatelle to me after the things in my line that I have done at the West. Do you begin to see through the plot?"

"Yes, and to blame myself for being so foolish as to give that desperate scoundrel such a chance to ruin me. Yes, I'll go back with you; I'll confront him, and ——"

"Slowly, Mr. Mulford. Brace yourself now for a shock. The half has not been told. The woman you love is true to you, or was, till your own willfulness put it in the power of a villain to lie her heart from you. Read this."

Another carefully restored letter he handed to the startled young man. The envelope bore the postmark of Bardwell, and it was addressed to himself at Bardwell — a drop letter. He looked at the date; it was the day next after that, two months before, when he had last seen the writer. He read the well-remembered, delicate characters, and a mist obscured his eyes. He kissed the paper passionately.

"O, how I have been deceived, betrayed!" he cried. "Was this, too, stolen and suppressed by the same bad hand?"

. "None other."

"Let us not delay a moment," exclaimed Mulford, rushing to the door and unlocking it. "For God's sake, good sir, let us hasten! I long to punish that scoundrel, and — and —"

The fervent desire to meet that beloved one from whom the basest villainy had separated him, was left unexpressed, but it throbbed eagerly with his heart.

"Hold, my dear young sir; you must know the whole truth. Bear what is coming like a man. I tell you there is that yet in this choice repository of crime that will wring your heart. There is also that which will stagger you with amazement. Summon your fortitude, now. Be a man, I say. Read!"

The speaker passed his arm about Mulford's shoulders, evidently fearful of the effect of the disclosure he was about to make. He had need to be. The young man took the tinted, cream-laid envelope, and withdrew the small sheet of similar paper from it, which bore several lines of print in copperplate script. His eyes devoured the contents at a glance. He turned a stony stare upon Mr. Lear, and the latter became aware that the man's whole weight was on his arm.

Ernest Mulford had fainted.

———

CHAPTER III.

TO THE RESCUE!

ELIAS LEAR laid his inert body down upon the lounge, and vigorously fanned the white, suffering face with his hat. In a moment the scattered senses returned, the eyes opened, and the sufferer sat up. He saw the detective standing by him.

" You are here, then ? " he said. " I have lived an age in the last five minutes. I hoped it was a dream."

" It is no dream, but a stern reality. Let us see if you can meet it like a man."

" Mulford's eyes fell upon the tell-tale invitation-card that had fallen from his hand. Snatching it up, he carefully read it again. A groan burst from his tortured breast.

" Lost — lost ! " he moaned. " *Half past eight o'clock of the evening of September 18, 1877!* It is *now;* this day; this very night! O pitying God, what shall I do? Man, whoever you are, have you brought me this cruel news only to torment me? What can I do? what can I *do*, I say! "

His voice was raised to a despairing cry, and he clutched the detective by the shoulder. Not in the least discomposed by his companion's words or manner, Mr. Lear consulted his watch. The minutes were speeding, the time was now twenty minutes before five.

"And you knew of this monstrous thing," continued Mulford, bitterly. "Yes, you knew it was to be; for here you have the notice of it, in black and white. And you did not stay at Bardwell, to stop it, as you might have done, but you must needs come posting off here to find me, and torture me with the ill tidings of what I cannot prevent. And you tell me you are my friend; and you ——"

Mr. Lear's hand was laid upon his shoulder. Something that he saw in those cold blue eyes told him to stop.

"I overlook your rashness and impatience," said the detective. "I know what you are suffering, and I sympathize with you; and I repeat that I have come here as your friend, and that you will soon be satisfied of it. But you have a right to know why I am here at this hour, instead of at Bardwell, when that document that you hold in your hand had warned me of what was to happen there, or near there, at half-past eight of this very night. Yes, I will tell you, since there is time."

He opened the door and called to the landlord.

"How is the horse?" he inquired, when the host appeared.

"Pretty stiff in the off hind leg, and sore in the flanks. Pardon, sir, but you used the whip on her pretty freely."

"I know it; I had to. Can she take two of us back to the station in an hour?"

"*No, sir!*" was the positive reply. "She's fed and watered well, but with the pull you've already given her, and taking into account this awful sultry weather, and there being two of you to go back—why, I say she can't do it. It would kill her."

"I may have to kill her then," said Lear. The landlord stared at him.

"Have her put to the buggy and brought round at once. Have you any wine in the house?"

"Some grape wine, sir."

"Bring me a large glass of it."

The detective returned to the parlor with a full goblet in his hand. Mulford was excitedly pacing the room.

"Drink this," said Mr. Lear. "Your nerves are all unstrung; you need a little bracing. This is a mild stimulant, and will do you good."

The young man swallowed it at a draught.

"The conveyance will be at the door in five minutes, and we will make a push to head off this magnificent rascal."

"Of what use?" Mulford cried. "What can we do at this late hour?"

"All — everything!" was the cheery response. "On the way here I studied the time-table and the train stops of this road, and everything is clearly laid out in my mind. I tell you, my boy, if the unexpected don't happen — and men of my business are always on the lookout for the dreadful unexpected — but if we have ordinary luck, we'll get there in time to-night, defeat that cunning schemer, make Mr. Ernest Mulford a happy man, and give Bardwell and vicinity such a sensation as has never been known there."

"Get there in time, to-night!" the other doubtfully repeated. "Impossible! I remember that the evening express is due at Bardwell a few minutes after nine. It'll all be over then; but by heaven, I'll meet him there at the station and kill him!" and the speaker clenched his fists.

"Young man, be quiet, and listen to me. I won't have any pistols or bloodshed about this affair; I've laid it out differently. I believe we shall have our smart gentleman inside the penitentiary before the first of January; but it will be by taking my way, not yours. Of course, I know what time the night express reaches Bardwell; that won't do for us, as you say. Eight miles this side of that village, as you know, is the little way-station of Drayton. Between those places runs the steep granite ridge, over which the highway is car-

ried on a very steep grade — too steep, the engineers
thought, for a railroad. That was thirty years ago,
when this road was first laid out; though I guess
engineering science wouldn't make much of it to-day.
And as the thick wall of granite could never be tun-
neled, they took the line around in a wide curve of
seventy miles, to a point where they could flank the
troublesome ridge."

"Yes," interrupted Mulford. "I know all this; but
I don't see ——"

"Patience!" said the detective, watch in hand. "The
train leaves Granby, over here, at six twenty-seven,
and stops five minutes on a siding at Drayton for the
down express to pass. It is due at Drayton at seven
fifteen; it is a flyer you know; from there to Bardwell,
around that immense curve, it makes every mile in a
minute and a half. But you see our problem, getting
off at Drayton, we want to make that eight miles to a
certain mansion just this side of Bardwell in sixty minutes, leaving us fifteen minutes' leeway after we get
there. Do you think we can get up that long hill and
over there in that time?"

"Horse ready, sir!" said the landlord, putting his
head inside the door.

"Very well; in a moment."

Ernest Mulford stood grasping the detective's arm
with both his hands, his eyes strained, his lips parted,
his face pale, as he hung on the other's words.

"We could do it; we will — if I can find Ted Vaun
there at the station. He's got a pair of strong blacks
and a stout democrat wagon; he can do it easily.
And Ted was my schoolmate; he'd do anything for me.
I tell you, sir, if we can get hold of Ted at Drayton
we are sure to be in time."

"We shall find him there," said Mr. Lear, quietly.
"All that a detective don't know and ought to know
he must pick up as he goes; and I learned all you have
told me about Vaun on the slow accommodation train

this morning. At Sunderland, twelve miles back, I telegraphed to him to be ready at Drayton Station, at seven fifteen, with his horses and wagon, promising him twenty-five dollars for a short ride; and to make sure that he would heed the dispatch, I put your name to it."

" Good — glorious!" Mulford shouted. " Now we're safe. Whoever you are, you are our savior, our noble benefactor; blessings on you, sir! — after this night is well over, we'll try to thank you. But come, now; let us be going."

" Yet a moment, Mr. Mulford. We must start fair; there is more yet that you must know; and," looking at his watch, which he had not returned to his pocket, " I see that I can spare two minutes to explain to you why I did not stay at Bardwell and stop the villainy of to-night, instead of coming here. It was simply because I first learned, upon the train that brought me here, what was going to happen at that house to-night."

" Why — why!" Mulford stammered. " Has it been kept secret?"

" The time — yes, remarkably secret. Interested as I have been in these affairs, and continually making quiet discoveries, I could not but see that the scoundrel was shaping everything to this supreme end. Yet you will remember that it is barely two months since you disappeared from Bardwell; and all the probabilities of such a case were naturally against haste and secrecy. But Weston Mayhew is cunning as well as unscrupulous; he is cunning as the devil, sir!—and that's the truth. Then he is immensely rich, as you know; I am satisfied that his figure is not short of two hundred thousand. What cannot such a man accomplish in the dark? If you ask his motive for all this secrecy, it can be easily explained. The dark paths that he has been lately treading, and the criminal acts that he has done, have made him fearful for his safety. What I am going to tell you in a moment will furnish the best reason in the world for his stealthy movements. I am satisfied that he does not mean to be seen in Bardwell after to-night. You stare—I tell you it is so. He knows that a storm is gathering over his head; he means to be west of the Rocky Mountains or beyond seas when it bursts. I learned yesterday what no one else in Bardwell knows: that he has forwarded his resignation as postmaster, and that he has turned his whole property into funds and securities. What does that look like? "

" Flight — and with *her* to share his disgraceful exile!" Mulford whispered. " If I miss him, may the vengeance of an insulted God overtake him! Yet, look at this card; here is publicity after all. How do you account for *that?* "

" Merely by supposing that there was a point beyond which poor deceived Emmanuel Gregory and his wife would not go, and that Mayhew had to concede this much to them. The information that I had been gathering for some weeks was at last amply sufficient to justify me in putting a sudden stopper on Mr. Weston Mayhew, and I resolved to wait no longer. But when the exposé was made, I wanted you there; in fact, you are a necessary witness as to the writing and posting of those letters. I knew where you were; nobody else at Bardwell knew, save Mayhew. The fact that you were so near probably hurried him up. But, much as I have unearthed of this man's villainy, I took my seat in the car this morning in profound ignorance of the crowning atrocity that he had contrived for to-night. This side of Drayton I overheard some of the conversation of two ladies about that invitation. Detectives are not often much surprised at anything; I *was* by what they said. They left the train at the next station, and the envelope and card were left on the seat in their haste. I secured them, read them, and thought very fast before the next station was reached. I found that I could not return to Bardwell by railroad before the night express, and that I should lose no time in continuing my journey. I picked up the information about Ted Vaun, got an opportunity to telegraph to him — and you know the rest. Only," and Mr. Lear's voice grew solemn and impressive, " we can see something in all this far beyond human contrivance. When I stepped aboard that train, the only human being who could prevent the outrage of to-night was ignorantly removing himself from the point of danger. The hand of Him who watches over the innocent was surely outstretched to throw that astonishing missive in my way."

He put on his hat and stepped into the hall. Mulford followed him. Mr. Lear paused, and took one more inclosure from the great envelope. It was of fine white paper, about the size of a bank-bill, partly written and partly printed. He held it up before the young man's eyes. It was quickly read.

" Just God," cried Mulford, " let him not escape us!"

The clock over the bar struck five.

CHAPTER IV.

ON THE TRACK.

THEY went out to the buggy. Mulford, in his eagerness to be off, jumped in first. With his foot on the step between the wheels, Elias Lear paused, hesitated, staggered back, and would have fallen but for the promptness of the landlord, who sprang forward and caught him.

" Are you sick, sir? " he asked.

" A little — I'm afraid," replied the detective, feebly. " Help me back to the parlor."

Ernest Mulford, seeing and hearing what had happened, got out and called a lounger to hold the horse. In the parlor he found Mr. Lear extended on the sofa, while the landlord's wife was wetting his head with a sponge. He smiled gravely as he saw Mulford, and the latter saw in his face that he wished him to come close. The young man did so, and sympathetically took his hand.

"This isn't dangerous, my dear fellow," he whispered. "I understand it perfectly. It's the after effect of a slight sunstroke. All this afternoon I have felt it coming on and have held it back by sheer force of will. I couldn't be sick, you know, till I had got you started on the right track. Go ahead now, and God prosper you."

"But I can't leave you in this way," Mulford protested.

"You can, and will. You can do me no good by staying here. You have heard nothing but the truth from me so far, and you shall know the truth about this. Three years ago, in Southern Missouri, I had just such a stroke at the end of such another hot day as this. 'You must be warned, Mr. Lear,' the doctor said, 'not to expose yourself long at a time to the direct rays of the summer sun.' At that time, perfect rest and quiet for twelve hours restored me, and I doubt not that they will do as much now. Go on; you've no time to lose. Don't worry for me. I shall follow you to-morrow morning and join you — somewhere."

"You'll let them send for the doctor?"

"Yes, of course, though I am sure that rest and quiet are the only physicians I need. Wait just a moment."

He closed his eyes wearily and seemed gathering strength to say more.

"Take the big envelope out of my pocket," he whispered again. "Take it along with you. I need not tell you to keep those papers as carefully as you would your heart's blood. Tons of gold could not buy them."

Mulford transferred the precious documents from the detective's inside pocket to his own.

"One last instruction," was faintly whispered. "Have you any money?"

" A few dollars."

" Take out my wallet. There are two thousand dollars in it, in large bills. Take half of it. You are starting on a mission, the length of which or the time of which no man can know. You can do nothing without money. Take it freely. I'll give you a chance by and by to account for it, and do you never stop nor rest till you overtake Weston Mayhew, and foil him."

It was not a time for quibbling or demurring. Mulford took the money, pressed Mr. Lear's hands, and hurried from the room.

Once more he sprang into the buggy. The landlord was at the horse's head, his broad red face overspread with a look of serious concern most unusual with him.

" You'll do everything for *him*, won't you? " Mulford asked, as he gathered up the reins, nodding his head toward the parlor. " You'll send for the doctor right off ? "

" O aye, sir; never you fear. Dr. Sumner lives just below here, and my old woman is the best nuss in the country."

" Let go," said Mulford.

" Just one thing, young sir. I don't want to blame the gentleman in there for hard driving; I see that some deviltry is afoot that you two are tryin' to head off; I see that, from the talk and actions of both of you. But the fact is, just the same, that poor beast has been shockingly put to it this awful hot day, and I tell you he ain't now in condition to travel three miles. And you're going to the station—and you mean to take the six twenty-seven west? "

" Yes," said Mulford, impatiently.

" What's the exact time now? "

" Quarter past five."

" Well, sir, you may do it; but you'll have a dead horse on your hands at the end of the road."

" Have you any horses? " Mulford demanded.

" No; and I dunno where you'd find one here."

" Then it can't be helped. Let go his head, will you? "

The landlord did so, and placed a small sponge and bottle at the young man's feet.

" There's some spirits," he said, " when he's ready to drop in the harness, sponge out his nose, and you may get a mile or two more outen him."

With a cut of a whip, the animal sprang away. The hamlet of Granby was quickly left behind, and the long, straight stretch of the road over to the station was before them.

For the first three miles the horse kept up a long trot without much urging. Then the whip had to be used to urge the tired limbs off from a walk. Short spurts of trotting slackened into a walk, and then into a dead halt. The heat at this hour was the most oppressive of the day. But for the powerful excitement that strung every nerve and muscle to action, Mulford would have sunk listless, like the poor dumb brute, under the burden of the sun and the atmosphere. As it was, he hardly noticed them.

Half the distance was passed. Far away eastward he heard a faint but prolonged note, shrill and clear, faint as it was.

" What's that? " he inquired of a man who leaned on his gate and fanned himself with his broad-leaved hat.

"" What? "

" That sound."

The rustic listened.

" Wal, I declare! Must be a mighty clear air to-day, if it *is* hotter 'n Tophet. That's the Western express whistling for Somers. I don't hear it more 'n three times a year."

" How far is it? "

" Twelve miles."

Mulford had ceased looking at his watch. He put on the lash. The horse sprang away; the lash was repeated; two painful miles were passed. Then there was a dead stop. The driver jumped out, filled his sponge from the bottle, rubbed it freely over the nose and head of the beast, and let him snuff the contents.

" You poor, brave creature!" he thought. " I do pity you; but I can't spare you, indeed I can't. "

Back in his seat, he urged the horse with his voice, and a fair speed was kept up for another mile. Then the pace slackened.

One mile and a half still lay between Ernest Mulford and Granby Station.

" It might as well be a thousand," he groaned, " with this miserable blown animal." ~

Another noise caught his ear. It was a faint rumble, a faint roar; and far off to the eastward he saw a tiny thread of black smoke lengthening out over the tree tops.

The express was near at hand on its rapid flight.

Unmercifully, unsparingly, now did he lay the whip on the quivering, smoking flanks of the stiff and ex-hausted animal. He snorted under the punishment, and with a wild neigh of fright broke into a gallop. The buggy swayed to and fro with the speed. The driver clutched the reins with one hand and laid on the lash with the other. With frantic bounds the horse sped along the dusty road. Mulford heard the clang of the bell, the rumble of the wheels, and, panting under the whip, the animal stopped at the rear of the station, and fell in the shafts.

Mulford got out and rushed around the building. The train stood on the track; there was some bustle and confusion. He saw three or four at the window buying tickets, and he stepped up there. Two or three more followed him.

" Drayton," he said, laying down a bill when his turn came.

The agent seemed almost bewildered by the unusual occurrence of half a dozen people wanting tickets for the same train. It was a rare thing at **Granby**. He seemed to want to say something to the man who had demanded a ticket for Drayton. He looked at him, and saw three other men pressing up behind him. He saw the conductor walking the platform, and knew that there could be but a moment more of delay, and he gave it up, or rather he handed Mulford his ticket and change, and in the pressure of the moment forgot what it was he was trying to say to him.

Mulford went out on the platform. A hand was laid on his arm.

" Your horse is dead, sir," said a man.

" I am sorry," said the young man, " but I had to crowd him. Who are you? "

" Simple Simon, sir, at your sarvice."

" Ah — the village expressman. Here — take this; bury the horse, and take care of the buggy. I'll be up this way again before long, and see you about it."

He turned away, leaving Simon in that excited state of mind that the gift of a five dollar bill would naturally produce upon him.

" All aboard!" the conductor shouted. The bell clanged. Mulford entered a car. The train was crowded; he procured a seat with some difficulty.

The sun had set twenty minutes before. The brief twilight was closing. The shadows of night were fast enveloping the familiar objects about the station as the train pulled out and gathered headway. Like a giant refreshed, the engine sped onward, faster and still faster, drawing its living burden of joy and sorrow, hope and fear, care and content. On, on, at full speed now, thundered the long train, with a rush and roar like the bellowing of some demon of the Arabian Nights let loose on earth; over rivers, along precipitous heights, through tunnels and past villages and farms, it fled at the rate of forty miles an hour. Sitting by the car window, watching the lights that flashed suddenly out of the darkness along the way and as suddenly disappeared, Ernest Mulford felt his heart bound and swell with the proud feeling of triumph yet to come, soon to come. He felt that he was to be vindicated; that the love of which he had been robbed by the most cruel villainy was to be restored to him; that swift and heavy punishment was about to descend upon the guilty. His heart, if not his lips, continually murmured:

"In time! — in time! — Heaven bring me there in time!"

———

CHAPTER V.

A DESPERATE EXPEDIENT.

"TICKETS!"

His eyes were bent upon the fleeting lights and shadows outside; he did not hear the familiar demand.

"Your ticket, sir, please."

The conductor's hand was laid upon his shoulder. He started, looked up at the bearded face of the official, which was becoming slightly clouded with vexation at the delay, comprehended what was wanted, and taking his ticket from his vest pocket, handed it over. The conductor took it, glanced at it, and looked with a frown at the passenger.

"Drayton," he said, snappishly. "*Drayton!* Well, I'll be hanged if some of these agents will ever learn anything. Did you get this at Granby?"

"Yes, sir."

"The stupid dolt! I told him myself, not twenty minutes ago, that Drayton was off the card for this train; that the new table was out, and he would have one to-morrow; and to be sure *not* to sell Drayton tickets for this train."

The conductor handed the ticket back.

"There's no help for it, sir," he said. "I'll take you on to Bardwell without charge, since you're not to blame, and you can come back by the accommodation in the morning."

He spoke quick and brusquely, as is often the way with his class, and passed on. He felt a hand on his arm, and looked over his shoulder. Mulford had risen up, and showed a white, rigid face to him.

" Sir," he asked, " do you mean to say that this train will not stop at Drayton to-night? "

" Well, that's about the size of it."

" I understood that this train waited there for the express east to pass? "

" It did yesterday; it won't to-night. They pass at Bardwell now."

" The public have had no notice of this, sir. Your agent sold me that ticket and took my money, without notice or explanation. I *demand* that you let me off at Drayton."

" O, come now, young man, don't put on airs. I guess I know what I'm about. This is disagreeable for you, to be sure, but you've got to stand it. I know my business and I shan't stop for you. So you take it cool. And I guess it ain't a matter of life or death with you, either."

" The happiness or misery of my whole future depends upon my stopping at Drayton to-night."

The words were spoken in a tone of such pathos that the conductor turned about and held his lantern up to scrutinize the face of the speaker. What he saw there impressed him.

" Wait a few minutes," he said; " I'll be back presently and I'll see what can be done for you."

At the rate of forty miles an hour the train rushed noisily through the darkness. After what seemed to Ernest Wolford an intolerable time, but which was only fifteen minutes, the conductor returned.

" Well! " he said.

A Sharp Night's Work 3

" I must stop at Drayton," was the decided statement of the passenger.

The people who filled the neighboring seats had become interested in the difficulty. Those who sat in front turned round, and those sitting back of Mulford craned their necks forward.

" I suppose you are strictly right," said the conductor. "The blunder of that lunkhead of an agent at Granby has given you the advantage. But I tell you kindly, sir, that I have my orders, and I *cannot* stop at Drayton."

" Cannot!" Mulford cried. "You have only to pull that bell-cord."

" If I did I might never have a chance to pull it after this trip," said the conductor, grimly. "In other words, I dare not stop. This is the first night of the new arrangement of the express trains meeting at Bardwell, and I must be on time. To lose the headway that this stop would cause, would make me ten minutes late there. I'm sorry for you, but I can't risk it. I must obey orders, and you can settle your grievance with the company."

" Is that all you've got to say to me?" Mulford asked. " I thought you said you would see what you could do for me. What made you say that? Look here, sir! I must and will leave this train at Drayton. If you refuse to stop it, I shall leave, just the same. Perhaps that will give you a better showing with the company! I call on these passengers to witness the outrage; this company sold me a ticket for Drayton, and now refuses to let me off there. And if I am carried to Bardwell to-night, untold misery to good people will be the consequence."

He became vehement, raising his voice till it rang through the car and sounded above the rattle and rumble of the train. Not I, reader, and not you, ever heard just such an appeal made in such a place; nor did we probably ever see a man possessed by such

intense and desperate agony of soul as fired that of
Ernest Mulford in that moment.   The nearest passengers looked sympathizingly at him; but, as is the way
of spectators in general of other people's distress, they
said nothing, and none of them ventured to interfere.

"Well, don't get huffy," the conductor said.   "I
will do all I can, all I dare to do for you.   I will slow
up as we pass Drayton, and — you can jump if you
want to."

"Good!" said Ernest, with deep relief.   "Excellent!   I thought you were a man.   I'll take the
jump."

"Mind, now; I don't tell you to jump!   I don't even
permit it; you're a fool if you do.   You'll take all the
responsibility."

"I make no bargain," was the reply.   "You are
bound to let me off at Drayton.   If you won't stop, I
shall get off the best way I can."

"You've good pluck, any way," muttered the conductor.   "You'd make a splendid railroad man."

The prolonged scream of the whistle and the clang
of the bell were at this instant borne back to them.

"That's for the road-crossing, three miles this side,"
he continued.   "If you're bound to leave at Drayton,
you'd better get out on the platform."

He hastened along through the car.   Ernest Mulford
rose and walked to the opposite end.   Unclosing the
door, he stepped out upon the platform.   Grasping the
rail with each hand, he descended cautiously to the
lowest step upon the side where he remembered that
the Drayton station stood.   A brakeman stood above
him with his hands on the brake-wheel, waiting for the
signal.

"It's going to be risky, sir," he shouted.   "We
can't check this speed enough to make it safe.   Better
not try it."

Mulford heard him, but gave no heed.   Tightening
his grasp on the rails, he leaned over and peered for-

ward. The roar of the train was in his ears, but he hardly observed it; he was not then, as at any other time he must have been, impressed with the fascinating peril of his position. There he stood, clinging to the rails, within eighteen inches of the solid ground, yet borne onward with such velocity that a single step at that moment would have hurled him into eternity!

He thought not of that; he thought not of death or danger; his yearning soul was speeding far in advance of the train, over the miles that still lay between him and the mansion just out of Bardwell.

The stars were dim in the sky; the landscape was rather obscure; the air was cool and refreshing after the intense heat of the day, and the rush of it fanned his face, now glowing with anticipation.

Familiar objects began to flit by. There was a lofty elm near by that he remembered; a white house, a half-burned barn.

The train passed under a road-bridge; he knew it well. He remembered the slight curve by which this station was approached. He peered forward again. There was the high light, plainly in view.

The whistle sounded in a prolonged shriek. He heard the rush of escaping steam. The brake-wheel crunched harshly behind him. He saw the end of the station and the platform before it coming into view.

Twenty car-windows were up, and eager eyes watched him. The passengers shuddered at the peril he was braving. They saw and knew what he did not — what he would not have heeded had he plainly seen and known it — that the speed of the train, although largely slackened, was too great for such an attempt. It could not have been much less than twenty miles an hour.

Opposite the door of the little station he jumped.

His feet struck the platform together. The impetus he had gained carried him two or three steps further, whirled him about and flung him over. He fell prostrate, his head striking heavily as he came down.

A LEAP FOR LIFE.—Page 36.

CHAPTER VI.

" NO SUCH WORD AS FAIL. "

THE train thundered on toward the ridge, and quickly disappeared in the woods that fringed its base.   Ernest Mulford lay still and senseless where he had fallen.

A short distance in rear of the station two men stood by the fence at the side of the highway.   One, a tall, strong fellow, in a blouse and overalls, held by the bits two spirited horses, that fidgeted uneasily as the train went by; the other, with his hands in his pockets, looked at the flitting phantom and heaved a deep sigh.

" Seems odd enough not to have the old flyer stop here," he said. " I came over only from force of habit to-night.   Nothing to do here.   What brought you, Ted?   You must have known this morning, when you got that dispatch, that your man couldn't stop here if the train didn't."

" Yes, I knew it.   Don't know what made me come. I expect it was my anxiety to do something, or try to do something to oblige Erny Mulford — God bless him! You don't know what a big-hearted fellow that is, Mr. Robbins, nor how he has helped me since we were at school together.   I want to be able to tell him, when I see him again, that I was here with the blacks to-night, all ready hitched up, waitin' for him, and willin' and anxious to serve him, if he could ha' stopped."

" What d'ye suppose he wants? "

" Well, I dunno, but I *guess* he wants to drop in on 'em over at Gregory's to-night."

The station-master gave a prolonged whistle.   The two as they talked had left the horses, which Ted Vaun had haltered to the fence, and walked over to the platform.   They were continuing their talk of what was about to happen at Mr. Gregory's, and what Mulford could mean by interfering, when they both at the same instant discovered the body of the latter where he had fallen. Hastily unlocking the door, the agent procured his lantern, lit it, and stooped down to examine the fallen man.

" Is he badly hurt? " Ted anxiously asked.

" Can't tell. It looks as though the fool had jumped off the flyer, and got the breath knocked out of him, any way. Bring him in here, and I'll look him over."

Ted lifted his friend bodily in his strong arms as easily as though he had been an infant, and, following the agent into his office, laid him down upon the lounge. They loosened his clothes and dashed some water in his face. Mulford groaned and opened his eyes.

" Where am I? " he asked. At Gregory's? "

" Oh, no! Erny; you're here at Drayton," Ted responded. " And I can tell you, my lad, you came pretty near being in Heaven, with your foolishness. "

" Take me on to Gregory's," Mulford murmured. " Don't delay a moment. Ted, drive your horses round here, and we'll get in. You must get there before half-past eight."

He closed his eyes wearily.

" I'm afraid he's injured internally," the agent said, passing his hands over his body and limbs. " Yet I don't see that any bones are broken."

The wandering senses of the sufferer were arrested by the words. He opened his eyes again, and with an effort that contorted his face with pain, he sat upright.

" My watch," he said. " Show it to me."

Ted took it from his pocket and held it up to him. The hands had stopped with the shock of his fall at seventeen minutes past seven.

" Mr. Mulford," the station-master interposed, " please lie down and be quiet. Do you feel any pain? "

" No; only a kind of faintness and a ringing in my head."

" Mighty lucky he didn't have concussion of the brain," the agent muttered to Ted. " It was a narrow escape."

"I say, Teddy," Mulford now eagerly demanded, "you got that telegram, didn't you?"

"Yes, Erny; but ——"

"And you've got your horses and wagon here, of course?"

"Yes; but you ——"

"Then let's start right away. I must be at Gregory's before half-past eight. You can make it, can't you, Ted?"

"O, yes; but you see ——"

He looked appealingly at the agent, who instantly interposed:

"Mr. Mulford, listen to me, and see if you can comprehend a little reason. I'm a bit of a doctor myself, and you are at present under my care. You have closely escaped a most serious, and probably fatal, injury, and your whole system has been severely shaken by the shock you have given it. Added to this, I see you are laboring under strong mental excitement. I tell you that the consequence of your going on to Bardwell to-night would, in all probability, be a brain fever. Do you comprehend?"

The patient looked at him, wearily but steadily.

"Yes, I comprehend; but I shall go, all the same."

The agent lost his temper.

"See here, sir; you don't stir a foot out of this building before morning. Lie down there, instantly. I'll give you an opiate and send over for Dr. Morton."

Ernest rose to his feet. He was weak and dizzy, and his legs trembled under him. Ted Vaun promptly threw an arm about him and held him up.

"You are very kind, Mr. Robbins," said Ernest, huskily, "and you mean to do the best you can for me, but you don't understand how I feel about this affair. I'll take no opiate! Sleep, sir! You want me to *sleep*, at such a time as this, when I alone can frustrate the plans of the wicked, and save helpless and deceived innocence? No, sir! I'll go to Mr. Gregory's with Ted if it kills me. I'd go if I *knew* it would kill me. Don't argue with me; don't try to dissuade me. Where's my hat? Teddy, help me out to the wagon. Good night, Mr. Robbins; a thousand thanks to you."

Before such a resolute spirit as this, speaking in the voice and shining out of the eyes of this heroic man, good Mr. Robbins weakened. He saw that all contention was useless, and bestirred himself to do the best he could for his stubborn charge. He was by Ernest's side before he could take a step.

" Just a moment," he said, with the utmost kindness in his voice. " If you're bound to go I won't try to detain you; but you must let me send you off a little refreshed."

" Time is passing; I can't wait," was the impatient reply. " For God's sake, let me go."

The agent took out his watch.

" Half-past seven," he said. " Ted, in how much less than an hour can you make it? "

The man switched some loose papers on the floor as he replied:

" It's a little short of eight miles to Gregory's. I can't rise the hill this side short of twenty minutes. After that, there's most six miles of beautiful down road. The blacks have done that, a mile in four minutes, many a time. Say fifty minutes, at the outside."

" That gives you ten minutes to spare," said the agent, briskly. " I want only one of those minutes."

He hastened to his desk, unlocked it, and produced a stout wicker flask.

" It is brandy," he said as he uncorked it. " I keep it here for sudden emergencies like this. Drink ! "

He offered it to Mulford, who put it away.

" Thank you, I never use it."

" But you'll take a good dram of it now," cried the agent, " or Ted shall hold you and I'll force it down your throat. Here you are suffering from a shock to your whole system, not fit physically to be out of bed, just about crazy yourself with nervous and mental excitement, and you're going to ride eight miles in an open wagon. Take it, I say, without any more fuss; I know what's good for men in your condition."

Ernest took a draught from the flask. The strong stimulant coursed through his veins and colored his cheek; he felt instantly strengthened and braced for the work before him.

Without further parley Ted Vaun led the way to his horses and unhitched them. Ernest climbed to the seat without assistance, and Ted was quickly by his side.

" Good-night," shouted Mr. Robbins, " and good luck ! "

" Good-night ! "

Ted gathered up the reins. " Hie up ! " he chirruped to his horses, and they reached out in a steady trot.

" Put on the lash ! " Ernest cried. " Teddy, my dear fellow, don't spare them."

" Don't fret, Erny. I know how to get speed out of these animals. The hill is only a quarter of a mile off; they'll get cleverly warmed up by the time they get to it, so they will climb like sailors."

" Do you mean to walk them all the way up that hill ? " Ernest cried, impatiently.

" Every step of it, my boy. Do you want me to run 'em up and founder 'em ? You keep cool, Erny; give me twenty minutes for the rise and then I'll spin you down the slope t'other side in a way that'll make you hold your hair on."

To the base of the hill the noble team went with a swinging trot. The driver held the reins in his left hand, while his teeth labored at an enormous plug of tobacco grasped in the other. His hat was drawn down to his eyes; his eyes were steadily bent on the road, over and beyond the horses' heads.

Ernest Mulford sat rather bent forward, also looking

ahead. His hand grasped the iron rim at the end of the seat; his heart throbbed madly; he took no heed of the pains that shot through his limbs and body. He was conscious of a strange exhilaration of spirits as he entered on the last stage of his journey. Every breath he drew was taken with an unuttered prayer that he might not be too late; each throb of his heart was audible. One thought, one aspiration, one prayer filled his mind, to the exclusion of all else —" O God of the helpless and the innocent, bring me there in time!"

And the wheels seemed to echo the prayer in their swift revolutions, the gentle night-breeze seemed to murmur it. Nature in her evening slumber seemed so full of sympathetic voices, that the words were continually ringing in his ears:

" In time, in time — O God, bring me to her in time!"

CHAPTER VII.

THE UNEXPECTED HAPPENS.

THEY reached the base of the hill. With long, even strides, without the least urging, the horses began to climb the steep and winding road. It was constructed up the rugged face of the jagged and irregular granite cliff where in many places the masses of rock had been blasted out to make foothold for man and beast. The way was painfully crooked; stunted trees growing in the clefts interrupted the starlight; this part of the journey was obscure and gloomy.

Ted Vaun discharged a copious libation of tobacco-juice over the wheel.

" How do you feel, Erny?"

" All right, Ted; but I can't talk. You say what you want to; don't mind me."

"O, well, my old chum, I guess I understand you. I've got to sing, or talk, or make some kind of noise in this pokery place. S'pose you think once in a while, Ern, about the times fourteen years ago or so when we sat on the same seat in the old school-house? You was a bright scholar, but I never could learn much out of books. Once you got a licking 'cause you wouldn't tell on me. By gum, Ernest, you was always plucky when you got roused! I used to think as long ago as that, that you had a kind of sneaking fondness for June Gregory, small as she was."

"Ted, don't! Don't mention her."

"O! aye, I see. What a lummocks I am, to be sure, to put my foot in it that way! Well, I'll talk about the horses; if you wa'n't along I should be talking *to* them. Perfect match, you see; six year olds. Wouldn't take five hundred of any man's money for em; both just as good as they make hosses, but David is a little, just a little, better'n Jonathan. Queer names? Yes. Well, I heard the minister one Sunday reading out of the Book about those two; how they was pleasant in their lives and in their death they was not divided, and I gave the names to the colts. You can't think now those creatures love each other! I believe if they were separated for a week, they'd pine to death."

Teddy's garrulous tongue ran on thus till the top of the hard hill was reached. As they passed the summit Mulford's eager eyes were strained ahead. The stars were shining brightly now, and he could see the broad descent sweeping with an easy grade down from the top of the ridge over miles of fertile territory. The highway stretched like a gray ribbon due west until lost in the distance, and six miles off lights were seen as they flashed out, disappeared and flashed again.

"Bardwell!" cried Mulford. "Now, Ted."

"Hie up, boys, hie-e-e there!"

At the driver's cheery, long-drawn cry the blacks broke into a fast trot, which in two minutes had increased to a tremendous pace. Faster, faster they went, the wheels spinning and the iron hoofs ringing on the road, while Ernest laughed and shouted with the long-pent pressure that must at last have voice.

And then—the unexpected!

A round granite bowlder, started by some heedless or reckless hand that day, had rolled down that smooth descent some fifteen hundred yards, stopping at last in the wagon-track.

The horses were right upon it; they saw it and swerved. It was upon Ernest's side; the driver never saw it. He heard the quick, warning cry of his companion, but he did not comprehend it. At that headlong speed one of the forewheels struck the great stone and was instantly shattered. The fore part of the wagon tipped down; the horses began to kick and bound furiously; with both hands did Ernest cling to the seat; how it was that he escaped death or frightful injury from those plunging hoofs he could not tell. He saw, in less time than it takes to say it, the horses free themselves from the gear and dash forward. Ted Vaun, holding like a vise to the reins, was dragged bodily from the seat and several rods along the road. With one leg fractured by a kick from one of those frantic hoofs the plucky fellow never released his grip of the lines, nor did he cease to cry " Whoa, Davey! So, Johnny!" in his efforts to calm the maddened team. They knew his voice, and, presently obeying it, stood still, though dripping with sweat and quivering in every muscle.

Ernest clambered out of the wagon and knelt down by his prostrate friend.

" Dear old Teddy," he said, " I hope you are not badly hurt?"

Ted struggled hard to repress his groans; but the pain was too much for him.

" No, I'm not much hurt, Ern. A few bruises, more or less—and Jonathan gave me a bad one on this leg."

"Can you get up? Let me help you."

He put his arms under Teddy's, and raised him. The poor fellow gave a cry of pain, and sank back.

"No use, Ernest. That leg's badly fixed; I can't stand. But you never mind. Get on one of the horses, and go on. Cut off the traces, strip the harness, and make a kind of bridle of the reins. Stick onto him, and give him his head, and he'll take you through. Don't mind me, old boy. Somebody'll come along here and pick me up soon; and it'll be no harm for me to lie on the ground awhile this warm night."

For a moment — for one unworthy moment, Ernest Mulford was tempted to comply.

One glance he cast far down the road toward Bardwell; one fierce clamor of his heart, to mount and ride away there, he resisted and overcame; and then he turned back to his helpless friend.

"Teddy," he said, "you can't think so meanly of me as to believe that I would leave you alone here in this way! I'm going for help, to that house that we passed back there. Will the horses stand — or shall I hitch them to the fence?"

"O, they'll stand; I'll talk to them. So, Davey! — quiet, John!"

Ernest ran swiftly back, and furiously assailed the door of the house. No one appearing promptly, he bolted in. The little place was filled by a laborer, his son, and their families; and the men, wearied with a hard day in the fields, were preparing for bed. Mulford burst in on them like a hurricane.

"Here! — come with me — I want you both," he exclaimed breathlessly. "There's a man hurt, out here; I want you to bring him in, and take care of him. Say — do you see *that?*"

He took a new fifty dollar greenback from his pocketbook and held it up to them.

"Why, yes, mister, we see it," said the elder of the two, "and a right good sight it is for sore eyes."

" Take it! " and the impatient Mulford threw it to
him. " Keep it; it's yours; only fly round lively, and
do what I tell you. I'll be back here in less than a
week; I'll give you another just like it. Will you do
as I tell you? — and make haste? "

" Why, bless you, yes; father and I'll do anything
for you. It's rare good luck you bring us."

" Listen, then; I've got to hurry away, and I want
you to do just as I say. There's two horses out here;
one of them I'm going to ride toward Bardwell; the
other I want one of you to mount and ride to Drayton
Station as though the devil had kicked you; find Mr.
Robbins, the station-master; tell him that Teddy Vaun
is out here with a broken leg; and then go to Dr.
Morton, and tell him to come here at once. Do you
understand? "

" O, aye, sir; we know both those gentlemen."

" And will you go? "

" I'll go, sir," the son spoke up.

" Well, now, take that door off its hinges; get a
mattress and put on it, and bring them out here to the
roadside. You've to fetch Teddy Vaun here, and put
him in you feather bed, and make him as easy as you
can till the doctor comes. The women here will do all
they can; I know they will. Hurry! "

He stood by, fretting and fuming, while the men
deliberately unhinged the door, and the women got the
mattress to lay on it. He walked the floor, showering
entreaties and imprecations on the heads of the men;
and they, used to the slow ways of day laborers, let him
storm, and took their time. At last they were ready;
and Ernest hastened out before them to where Vaun
lay on his back. He was talking to the horses, and a
whinny occasionally showed that he was understood.

" O, is that you, Erny?" Vaun said. " What do you
think? — just now Jonathan came round here and put
his head down to me, same as to say he was sorry.

Poor fellow, he was frightened; he never meant it. But say — ain't it high time you was off?"

"Yes, Ted. These folks will take good care of you. I'll come round in a few days to look after you. Good-by, Teddy."

"Good-by, Ern. You'll get there. O, I say — take David?"

"Yes."

Ernest Mulford took the laborer's son aside.

"Take that horse to your shed, so you will have him secure," he said.

The man started with him. Mulford removed all the harness from the other horse, and extemporized a bridle out of the lines.

He found himself growing weak. He had to lean against the horse to keep himself up.

"Help me to his back?" he said.

The laborer did so.

"Now head him toward Bardwell."

It was done.

"Stand clear!"

He crouched down upon the bare back of the animal, turning his knees closely in, and held a loose rein. He had not the strength to sit upright. With a strap cut from the harness he gave the horse a cut over the flank. The spirited creature bounded, snorted and bolted down the road like a shot.

The laborer's son had now returned, and stood with his father, watching the shower of sparks struck from the stony road by the iron hoofs of the vanishing horse.

"A dreadful rattle-brained chap," the son remarked, gaping after him.

"Very free-like of his cash," said the elder of the two, fingering the substantial reality of a fifty-dollar note.

Ted Vaun was growing delirious. Their voices

roused him and summoned back his lingering consciousness.

" Where is he? " was his question.

" Vamoosed with one of the horses."

" Which one? "

" The one with the half-cropped ear," replied the laborer.

" Aye," whispered Vaun, " that's David; he'll take him through."

And as they bore his poor, bruised body to the house, they heard him softly murmur the last words that he spoke in consciousness for days:

" David is a leetle — just a *leetle* — the best of the two. He'll do it, if either of 'em could! "

CHAPTER VIII.

THE LAST RALLY.

AWAY, now, as if on the wings of the wind! No further need to use the strap: a word, a cry, and the great black horse, with the sinews and wind of a Centaur, increased his speed. With a gallop like a whirlwind he tore along the highway, neighing and snorting in the fierce joy that the rapid motion gave him. And, clinging to his back, weak, almost delirious, and still holding on with the clutch of desperation, the rider repeated his cry:

" Faster, David — faster!"

Several wayfarers were passed on the road. They looked with terror and superstition at this phantom horse and rider, appearing and disappearing in a whirl. Two or three carriages on the way abandoned the road in time to escape being ridden down and demolished.

Nearer and nearer flashed the lights of Bardwell. He was almost there.

A Sharp Night's Work 4

Yet, as he rode, in the clear air which on that night conveyed sounds to a great distance, he heard a sound that struck terror to his soul.

Far away to the north, faint but shrill he heard the shriek of a whistle.

Too well he knew what it meant! The night express west had rounded the great curve, and was coming into Bardwell.

" Faster, Dave — faster!"

The iron hoofs clattered on the stony road. Nearer, very near to the village he came.

But steam moves faster yet; and he was a good half mile away when he heard the rumble of the train. Nor had he reached the village when he distinctly heard the clinging of the engine-bell, mingled with the first heavy puffs as the train drew out.

" God strengthen me! — God keep *her!* " he prayed.

Bardwell at last. Its lights were right before him. Here, at the end of the long, straggling, elm-shaded street, and somewhat beyond it, he saw a well-known mansion by the roadside, but well back from it. A large two-story frame house of antique architecture, surrounded by wide lawns and gardens. Along its front was a white-pillared portico. He saw the house ablaze with light; for the air was so mild that the blinds had been flung open. Not only light, but laughter, music, and the pleasant hum of voices came forth. Many figures appeared through the windows. In the grounds, among the fountains and shrubbery, couples were strolling, chatting, and flirting. All was lightness and gayety.

So much he saw as he dashed up to the gate, threw himself off, and rushed in.

The promenading couples then saw a sight that sadly frightened them.

A man with wild eyes, pale face, and disordered hair, rushed up the walk to the front door. His coat was torn half way up the back; his clothes were dusty; he was bare-headed. Women shrieked and ran from him; men silently fell back.

The strange apparition burst into the great double parlor. The falling of a bomb-shell through the roof could not have caused greater consternation. A quadrille just formed was broken up and scattered. Some of the company fled from the room; others sought the corners, or got behind the furniture.

He leaned upon a chair.

"Where is my Uncle Gregory? — and my aunt?" he huskily whispered.

A florid old gentleman in a blue swallow-tailed coat, with ruffles at breast and wrists, came cautiously forward.

"Why, its Ernest!" he exclaimed.

"Ernest!" echoed a hale old lady, advancing. "So it is! O, deary me, what is going to happen? O, Erny, Erny, how could you? To think that my own sister's son would act so!"

The tender-hearted soul began to cry. But her husband frowned.

"Nephew," he sternly said, "your conduct is outrageous. What do you mean by intruding here at such a time, and after what we have all suffered on your account? Why did you not return a month ago, beg forgiveness of your excellent employer, and of your relatives whom you have shamed, and so fit yourself to attend here to-night? What d'ye mean, sir, by coming in this condition? Are you drunk or crazy? — or what *is* the matter with you? Speak!"

This fine burst of reproach was thrown away on Mulford. His eyes wandered round the room, and through the open doors, crowded with terrified but curious faces, looking for one whom he did not see.

"Uncle Gregory," he said, "Aunt Jerusha—where's June?"

"O Lordy!" the plump and rosy old lady cried.

" I *know* something is going to happen! Ernest, you
dear boy, what makes you act so? "

" Where is June? " he shouted.

" She's gone with her husband," replied Mr. Gregory.
" What have you got to say about it? "

Ernest clutched the back of the chair.

" Gone! — husband? " he vacantly repeated.

" Yes. She was married right here, at precisely half-
past eight, to Mr. Weston Mayhew, and they're on their
way to New York this minute, on their wedding tour."

" Ernest, please go up-stairs to your old chamber and
lie down," his aunt pleaded. " Don't — please don't
make a scene here to-night before all these people."

He heard her words, as he had heard those of his·
uncle; but the only fact that he distinctly comprehended was that the blow had fallen; that he had come
too late; that crafty and powerful villainy had triumphed,
and that June was lost to him forever. He staggered
in front of the great chair and sank down in it.

" Lost! — ruined! — the innocent prey of a black-
hearted scoundrel! " he moaned. " God help her —
and me."

A profound silence followed his words. The heart-
rending pathos of his tone impressed everybody. The
hush of direful expectation fell upon the assemblage; all
knew that something terrible was about to be disclosed..

" What do you mean, sir? " Mr. Gregory thundered.
" It's unmanly for you to come here in this way, after
Mr. Mayhew has married June and started on the
wedding journey, and try to blacken his character by
such miserable insinuations. What do you mean? "

" *I mean that he is a bigamist!*" Mulford cried.

The silence of consternation fell upon the assemblage.

" He is the most infamous of men," the young man
pursued. " I never did a wrongful act; he has blackened
my name to you all. He has stolen and suppressed letters; he has forged letters; he has won June Gregory by
the bas⌐?t trickery and fraud ; he has had for months

another wife living in a town sixty miles from here, and but this very afternoon I learned the shocking truth. Through such dangers and trials as can not be now recounted I have striven to reach here in time, and snatch poor June from the contamination of his hand. I have failed; I am baffled for the time; but mark me! — that rich and powerful villain shall not triumph long. God will yet keep June from his unclean clutch. I will save her, though I die at her feet!"

He sank exhausted in the chair.

CHAPTER IX.

THE EVIL EYE.

BETWEEN the sunset and the twilight of an evening in the previous July, a man stood in the doorway of a store on the principal street of the village of Bardwell. He stood in a comfortable, half-lounging attitude, his fingers playing with the ornament upon his heavy gold watch-chain. He was of medium height, thick-set, but still active and quick in his movements. He was fashionably, almost foppishly, dressed ; and a single glance would have shown that he was of a different order from the general run of country village people. His full brown face was smooth-shaven; a comfortable double chin depended from it. His hair was thin at the top, and brushed carefully so as to conceal the tendency to baldness. His features were small, and seemed almost lost in the grossness of the fat face. His eyes were black and restless, roaming quickly from one object to another; and when they happened to become riveted upon a person, they were as keen in expression as those of a hawk. His age was something between forty and fifty. Over his head, his name in full shone upon a large sign in gilded letters:

Weston Mayhew.
General Merchandise at Retail.

By the side of the large doorway was a smaller tin sign:

Post Office.

We have briefly described the foremost citizen and wealthiest man of this village. Few there were in Bardwell who were able to say that they personally liked the man; but the collective opinion of the people about him could not have been other than highly favorable, for he did the largest and most thriving business in the place. Anything that the people needed could be bought at his counters, from a paper of pins to a cook-stove. He was the village postmaster. He was a deacon of the leading church, superintendent of its Sabbath-school, and sang in its choir. Men bowed low to him, women smiled sweetly upon him; he was all wrapped up in the praise and the general esteem of this people.

Ten years before this time he had come here from the far West, unknown, unintroduced, and had at once taken a firm grasp on the business and social life of the place. Nothing was known of him by the Bardwell people more than what he had shown them; they knew absolutely nothing of his past life. Indeed, there was that in his secret life here that would have shocked and horrified them, could they have known it; because the man was in fact a whited sepulchre, fair outside, bnt vile and evil within. The cloak of religion and extensive and honorable dealing that he had assumed covered a thoroughly bad heart, willing and ready to prey on society, and ever watching for a safe and tempting opportunity.

As he stood there in his store door on this evening, an opportunity was presented to him.

At this hour June Gregory came out from the com-

fortable home of her foster parents, and walked down
the street.   She was·just nineteen, rounded and grace-
ful, with sunny hair, bright eyes and glowing cheeks.
She walked on in maiden innocence and loveliness,
presenting, with her simple summer dress and ribbons
and light hat, a picture so fair that even those who had
always known her turned when they had met her and
received her smile, looked back, and said in their
minds, " How beautiful."

In the mild and flowery June of a year nineteen
years gone, a little infant had been laid in a basket
upon the doorstep of the Gregorys.   They were child-
less ; one after another their darlings had been torn
from them by cruel disease.   Their hearts warmed to
this helpless waif, and she had been brought up as their
own.   Of her parentage nothing was ever discovered.
Nor did these kind people care to know about it.   She
came to them as a blessing, and daily for years she
had grown closer to their loving hearts.   A card
pinned to the blanket that was tucked about the little
body, bore the words, in a delicate female hand, " Her
name is June."   So she was called; and she seemed
to have borrowed, with the name of the month of her
nativity, something of its brightness, its beauty and its
bloom.

She walked on until she reached Mr. Mayhew's store,
and turned to enter it.   The proprietor bowed; she
smiled and nodded in return, and passed in.

What was it that then, at that moment, arrested this
man's attention, drove for the time everything from his
mind but her image, and filled him with something like
a frenzy for her possession?

Who can tell the ways or the works of the heart of
man — of the wolfish heart of the bad man?

An hundred times before had he met this girl,
beginning with the days when, as a school-girl of nine,
he saw her pass along the street, laughing and frolicking
with the other children.   He had observed, as he

observed a thousand other things which at the time made no sensible impression upon him, that June Gregory was growing to womanhood, and was developing into a wonderfully lovely girl.   He had given her just that general admiration that female beauty obtains from all men.   An hour before he probably would have resented it angrily had any one said to him, " You're quite fond of pretty June, aint you, Mr. Mayhew?"

But as she passed him there and entered his store, a sudden inordinate passion for her sprang into existence in his breast.   Perhaps it had been secretly gathering there for months, and perhaps the little smile she gave him, just as she would have smiled upon any male acquaintance, inflamed his fancy and quickened his desire.   We do but record the fact, without seeking to explain it, that at that instant a passion for this girl seized upon him with the grip of a lion.

He turned and looked after her, as she went to the counter behind which Ernest Mulford stood.   And in his bad heart he registered an oath.

" I'll have her — by God, I'll have her! "

He knew that he had no right thus to look upon or to think of her.   He knew, as others did not know, the sacred legal barrier that stood in the way of the possession of this fair prize, even if he could win her heart. He knew, but he cared not.   Duty, honor, conscience were thrown to the winds; the man was thenceforth given over to the devil!

CHAPTER X

THE COURSE OF TRUE LOVE.

ERNEST MULFORD'S eyes brightened as she approached.   They exchanged the usual greetings of young people who are well acquainted; and then June requested to be shown some small articles in the line of female dress.

He showed her the goods; she looked at them, they chatted about them, and the best part of half an hour was consumed in the purchase. Two or three people came in and went to the post-office, which was kept at the back end of the store. Ernest looked toward the door, and seeing that Mr. Mayhew showed no signs of coming back to wait on them, he excused himself to June, and went and attended to them. Returning, he put up her purchases in a very small package, received the pay for them, and heard his customer's " good evening."

" Wait!" he said in a low tone, leaning forward. "Are you going home now?"

" Yes."

" It's about time to close. Mr. Mayhew is here, and the evening is so fine that I don't care if I walk along with you. May I?"

The girl gave a little coquettish toss to her head.

" O, I don't care," she replied.

Women have ever been a mystery, since time began, and will not cease to be till the end of time. For months, yes, for years past, that kind of actions which speak louder than words, had assured this girl that this man sincerely loved her. That he had never told her so made no difference with the certainty that she felt on the subject. And she was not indifferent to him. If, on the one hand, she had never in her hours of self-examination brought her heart to confess that he was its master, on the other hand she did know that she warmly regarded him; that she liked him far better than any other man of her acquaintance.

Naturally, this state of mind would lead her to a complete surrender of her heart to him. Perhaps she would have given it up to him on the asking, on any evening but this.

And why not on this evening?

Reader, do you know what it is to be *perverse?* Have you ever felt strangely drawn to do what you did not wish to do; to say words that you regretted as soon as they were spoken?

Such moods are common to mankind; they are far more common to womankind. Why they seize us, why it is that we permit ourselves to yield to them, are of the mysteries that fill our earthly life.

In such a frame of mind as this was June Gregory upon that night. Something told her that Ernest Mulford was about to declare his affection for her, and she capriciously set herself against him.

He took his hat and accompanied her to the door. Mr. Mayhew looked at them as they passed. Nothing of his feelings showed in his face.

" I would like to leave a few minutes before time, sir, to-night," Ernest said. " If you'll lock the door, I'll return in an hour, and set everything to rights for morning."

The merchant nodded. As they slowly passed up the street, side by side, he looked after them. A suspicion of the truth entered his mind. With it came ungovernable jealousy, and the determination that if this man, his faithful clerk, who had served him with rare zeal and industry for some years — that if he should presume to come between him and this girl, he would ruin him and drive him from the village!

The couple walked on together for some minutes, making only casual remarks, allusions to the little news of the town, such topics as the projected Sabbath-school picnic, the coming party, and so forth. All this was quite foreign to the subject that lay very close to Ernest's heart, and more than once, as they walked, he tried to introduce that subject. Divining his intention with woman's quickness, June always checked with rene.ved small-talk his efforts to speak his heart.

But i.ª had made this opportunity, for he was determined to ᴜave his say this night. When, therefore, they had reached the gate at Mr. Gregory's lawn, and she quickly bade him good-night, without asking him to come in, his hand detained hers.

There they stood, face to face, with the gate between them: typical, although they did not know it, of the strong, hard barriers that fate or chance — who can tell which — was building up between them. Nor did they know that over that same gate the pair who were now prosaic old man and wife in this mansion had done *their* wooing, when, years before, the young and dashing Emmanuel Gregory had come to tell his story to the only daughter of the house.

" One would really think, June," said Ernest, boldly taking the plunge, " that you cared less for me than for anybody else. If it is not so, I don't know what you mean by all this coolness."

" Really!" the girl said, with a little forced laugh, " who told you that I cared a button for you? Aren't you presuming a good deal to-night, Mr. Impertinence?"

" It is high time I knew what you *do* think of me. June, let me ask you the question squarely: Do you love me?"

" No."

She said it with a pout. He turned his face sharply away, to hide what was in it.

" That is—" she added. There was a full stop. He turned again, his dashed-down hopes revived by those two words.

" Well, June?"

" What do you want me to say?" she pettishly rejoined. " I don't see what right you have to talk so."

" You have answered my question, June; but I don't want to take such an answer. Do you really mean it?"

" She cast down her eyes, while the rich color mantled her cheek.

" Why, Ernest, to be frank with you, I hadn't

thought of such a thing. We've grown up together from our school days, and I never looked on you as anything more than a real nice friend. Then you're so much older than I am."

" Less than seven years."

She was silent. She was really thinking of something to say that would encourage him, while it should not be a complete yielding on her part.

" June, this is a very anxious hour for me." He spoke with a deep seriousness, and she glanced shyly, but with secret admiration at his eloquent eyes. "Perhaps I understand you. Because I have been so much here at this house, where my good aunt and uncle have always treated me as affectionately as if I were their own son, have you thought that I cared to be nothing more to you than a kind of brother? It is not so. I have always loved you; and since you have become a woman grown, I have looked with fear lest some one should come and take you from me. Not now, June — not this month or this year — but, some day, will you be my wife?"

She had broken the stem of a rose from a bush close at hand, and now pulled off the leaves as she listened. She laughed again.

" That ' some day ' was well put in, Mr. Mulford. I'm afraid it would be a pretty long day, though I'm young enough to wait. But you are nothing but a poor clerk ——"

She stopped abruptly, abashed by the flush of pain, mortification and anger that her unthinking taunt sent to his cheek.

" Say no more, June," he said, with unfeigned bitterness. " I have made a mistake, a sore one for me; but it is better for me to learn it now. I shall never speak to you again on this subject. May God bless you! "

He threw his arms about her, kissed her, and hurried away.

Almost before she could comprehend what had happened she was alone. She leaned over the gate, and
looked down the street. He was hidden by the gath-
ing shadows of the night.

Then her heart spoke out, in spite of herself.

"Ernest! Ernest! Come back!"

He did not hear her. What misery might have been
prevented, what stirring scenes, recorded and yet to be
recorded, would never have occurred had that gentle and
sorrowful voice penetrated a little further into the night.

She lingered a moment, and then hastened into the
house. Mrs. Gregory met her in the hall.

"Why, June!" she said. "Whatever is the matter
with the child? If you haven't been crying!"

She would not trust herself to answer, but ran up-
stairs and locked herself in her room.

When midnight came, and that house and all the
houses in Bardwell were still in slumber, the remorseful
girl was still sitting by her little table, her head bowed
upon her hands.

Woman's love had been fighting a hard battle with
woman's pride, and the former had won.

She took some stationery from the drawer and wrote
a letter. We must look over her shoulder as she writes.

July 13th.

DEAR ERNEST—I am dreadfully afraid and ashamed
to write those two words; but if you had stayed with
me only a minute more, you would have made me say
them to you. What made you rush away so? You
are angry with me; you must not be angry with poor,
foolish me. Did I say something to hurt your feelings?
What was it? I forget what we were talking about.
You may come over to-night (it is past midnight now,
and I have been sitting up ever since you were here),
but you must not kiss me again. That is, unless I tell
you that you may.   JUNE.

She pressed her lips to the letter, closed, directed

and stamped it. With a sigh of satisfaction she laid it on the table.

She had but just risen to prepare for bed, when a sudden thought made her heart flutter.

"How nice it would be for him to get it the first thing in the morning!"

She acted instantly on the thought. Putting on her hat and a light shawl, she silently descended the stairs, let herself out at the front door, and ran down to the gate.

She looked along the street. It was absolutely still and deserted.

There was a bright moon in the sky. The distance was a third of a mile to the post-office; but she did not hesitate.

With swift feet she sped along the way, and reaching the place, dropped the letter into the slit in the door. Then, with wildly beating heart, but with a deep sense of satisfaction, she sped home. Nobody had seen her, nobody knew of her mission.

Ah! — one person there was who knew of it.

She did not look behind her when she hastened away from the post-office door. Had she done so, she would have seen the door softly unclose, and the distorted face of Weston Mayhew thrust out in the moonlight. The letter she had just posted was held in his hand!

CHAPTER XI.

THE TRAIL OF THE SERPENT.

AT EIGHT o'clock Mr. Mayhew locked the store. But instead of locking it as usual from the outside, he locked it from the inside. Going back to his desk, he turned up the gas, and, sitting down in his large chair, he became immersed in thought. His home was at a neighboring hotel; but he cared not to go there now. He wanted to think.

To think — about June Gregory. The sight of her beautiful face and form that evening, connected with his evil resolution, had completely absorbed him. He had already began to plan for the accomplishment of his design. Many obstacles he saw in the way, but he determined to overcome them. He resolved to crush everything that might come between.

Almost an hour he had sat there in deep meditation, when he heard a key rattling in the lock. He knew that it could be none other than his clerk. The desire to spy upon his actions swiftly entered his brain. It came to him because he was thinking of June, and he had seen his clerk accompanying her home upon terms of apparent intimacy.

He remembered that the gas in the office — part of the store could not be seen from the street, so that the person who was about to enter had not yet seen it, and he turned it out. Then, for greater precaution, he crouched low behind the desk. He heard the door open and close.

He heard the uncertain movements made by hands and feet in the dark; the scratching of a match; the rush of released gas, and then there was a light in the middle of the store.

By peering out by the side of the desk, he was able easily to see Mulford, and watch his movements.

He saw him go behind the counters, put up on the shelves some rolls of goods that had been left down, and then move about, putting the store to rights.

As he passed here and there near the gaslight, the concealed watcher saw his face, and observed with surprise that it was sad and overcast.

What could that mean? Little more than an hour before, he had walked away with June in excellent spirits. What had happened to so depress him?

Nor was this all. Once, as he came nearer, the man in hiding plainly heard a deep sigh.

Never suspecting that he had been watched, Ernest

left the store, locking the door after him. Mr. Mayhew relit the gas and resumed his cogitations.

Much absorbed he must have been, for he was aroused by the clock striking one. He turned down the gas again, put on his hat, and started for the street.

He was just about to insert his key into the lock, when he heard the rattle of a letter in the tin box on the door.

No man can account for his sudden impulses. Weston Mayhew could not have told what caused him to take out the letter and light a match to read the address.

He read the name of his clerk on the envelope, written in a woman's hand. He quickly and softly unclosed the door and looked out. The street was light and he easily recognized the figure that was rapidly flitting away.

He reclosed and relocked the door, returned to his office, lit the gas again, and placing the letter on the desk, sat down and looked steadfastly at it.

We have said that this man was bad at heart. He had within him great possibilities of vice and wickedness, hidden under a garb of hypocrisy. Yet, thus far, he had avoided crime. Not that he was not bad enough; the very worst of men never lay themselves liable to the heavy hand of the law. It was, in Weston Mayhen's case, only because he had never yet been sufficiently tempted.

The temptation lay there before him.

But one other beside himself knew of the mailing of that letter. That other was the writer. He could open, read and destroy it; he could learn from it the footing upon which his clerk stood with the woman whom he had resolved to possess, and nobody would be the wiser.

He did not try to resist the temptation; he did not care to resist it. There, in the silence and secrecy of the night, he violated honor, duty, and his oath of office, and for the first time became a criminal. He tore open the envelope and read the letter.

He read the tender, touching words, fresh from the heart of the writer, yet spiced with maiden coquetry.

A fearful curse broke from his lips. He tore both sheet and envelope into minute pieces, and threw them into his waste-basket.

He got up and strode back and forth through the store. The black frown that covered his face gradually gave room to an expression of deep thought. Suddenly he clapped his hands and laughed aloud. If evil spirits can make themselves heard they might laugh that way.

" I'll do it ! " he said. " By heaven, I believe it will work ! "

He took the office letter-book from the desk and turned, one after another, to several copies of his clerk's letters.

" She may and she may not know his hand," he muttered. " It is best to be safe."

Mr. Mayhew was an expert penman. He was well acquainted with the general character of Ernest's chirography, and could at once make a fair imitation of it ; but he labored carefully and systematically over this, his first forgery. He finally satisfied himself with the following production:

JULY 14.

MISS GREGORY: I have received your letter, and I am much surprised by it. If you think that you can put me on and off in this way, according to your whims and caprices, then you do not know me. I have very good cause of offense, and I am tired of the treatment you give me. You will please consider everything at an end between us. ERNEST MULFORD.

Mr. Mayhew held this precious document up to the
A Sharp Night's Work 5

light and laughed and chuckled over it, reading it over
and over again.   Then he thought again.

"He could hardly tell it from his own writing," he
soliloquized.

He folded it, enveloped and carefully directed it,
and placed it in his drawer, not forgetting to turn the
key on it.   Then he went to his lodgings.

It was Ernest Mulford's habit to open the store
promptly at seven o'clock, get everything ready for
the day, and await the appearance of the proprietor,
who usually came in about half-past eight, when the
clerk went to his breakfast.

The night that had just passed into a new day had
been a sleepless and sorrowful one for poor Ernest.
He was up before six, bathing his aching head and
heavy eyes.   Restless in mind and body, he left his
boarding-place and went over to the store.   For the
moment he forgot his grief in the astonishment of
finding the store open, and Mr. Mayhew inside.   The
proprietor met him near the door.   The "good-
morning, sir!" with which the clerk greeted him was
met by a cold and severe face.

"You need not take off your hat, Mr. Mulford.
Your engagement here is at an end.   In this envelope
you will find the amount of your wages for the
month — up to the last of the present month — which I
think is a very large concession to you, *after what has
occurred.*   I wish you a good-day."

He turned on his heel, and walked away.   Almost
stunned with this new distress, Ernest slowly followed
him.

"Mr. Mayhew!"

The merchant turned sharply.   "Well?" he snapped
out.

"May I ask how I have displeased you?"

"You *are* a good one!" was the sarcastic answer;
and Mr. Mayhew elevated his dark eyebrows.   "As if
you didn't know!"

" I don't know, sir. "

" Take care, young man! You may anger me into making this a public affair. "

" For God's sake, sir! — for my sake! — tell me what you mean. You know I have served you for years. "

" I do know it, to my sorrow. "

" Do you mean to blast my good name here, where I am best known? "

" If you don't make too much fuss, and drive me to an exposure, I shall not stand in the way of your leaving town as soon as you please. I promise nothing further. "

The unhappy young man put both hands to his head.

" Do you mean to say that I am dishonest? "

" I haven't said it yet; but since you ask the question, you shall have a plain answer. Yes! — I do. "

Ernest turned and left the store without another word. It was not yet seven o'clock. He walked along the street, meeting nobody at that early hour that he knew. He looked up, and saw that he was passing Mr. Gregory's place.

The old grief came back to his heart. The darling hope that he had cherished for years had been rudely destroyed. He could not remain here now, seeing her every day, and ere long seeing some other win and wear her.

The crafty devil in the breast of Weston Mayhew had exactly timed the cruel stroke that had just been dealt this man. None knew him better than his employer; he was a judge of human nature. He saw that Ernest was suffering deeply from slighted love and wounded pride, and he had planned still further to crush his spirit. At another time the faithful clerk, conscious of his own rectitude, would have indignantly hurled back Mr. Mayhew's insinuations and boldly dared him to the proof. In the state of mind in which this morning found him, his employer's words were terrible to him. He knew not what was behind them; he feared that

some plausible case had been made against him.   He
could not conjecture what motive Mr. Mayhew could
have for trying to ruin him.   In fact, he was indifferent
as to the motive.

In a few hours the home of his boyhood, his
youth and his young manhood had become insufferable
to him.   He determined to abandon it forthwith.   In
the bitterness of his spirit he resolved that he would not
even spend a few hours in bidding farewell to his
friends and acquaintances; not even to his good aunt
and uncle.   He would not even return to take the cars
at Bardwell.   So he hastily, rashly, resolved, as he
stood in the cool of the morning, looking at Mr. Gregory's house.

" Farewell, June!" he murmured.   " Other men will
love you; they cannot help that; but not as I have.
We shall never meet again."

He dashed the tears from his eyes, and walked on.
He thought of some little debts that he owed at Bardwell, and of his trunk at his lodgings.

" I will go off to some obscure place," he thought,
" fix these things by correspondence, and make up my
mind what quarter of the world I want to strike for.
All lands ought to be alike to me now."

Toward evening of that day Mr. Mayhew heard indi-
rectly from his discharged clerk.   He saw a man who
told him that he saw him board the accommodation
train at Drayton that morning.

Mr. Mayhew turned away and chuckled.

People wondered at the absence of Ernest, and
inquired of the merchant where he had gone.   And
the merchant mysteriously shook his head, and sometimes said, with a sigh:

" I don't wish to injure him.   I'd rather say nothing
about it.   Ah, I feel sad for that fallen young man!"

On the morning of the next day after Mulford's disappearance, Mr. Mayhew took the forged letter from
his drawer, stamped it with the Bardwell post-mark,

and placed it in Mr. Gregory's box.　June herself came
to the postoffice about noon, and received it from his
hands.　When she had gone, Mr. Mayhew, being
alone, broke out into boisterous mirth at the success of
his scheme.　The devil in him was roaring loudly!

CHAPTER XII.

THE DETECTIVE APPEARS.

THE month of July went past at Bardwell.　Early in
August the evening train from the West brought,
among others, a stranger to the place.　He rode over
to the hotel in the omnibus, registered the name
"Elias Lear," and being wearied with a long, warm
and dusty day's travel, he retired early.

At breakfast the next morning he was seated opposite Weston Mayhew.　The two men took keen notice
of each other, without seeming to do so.　As the meal
progressed, had the thoughts of each been put into
speech, they would have been something like this:

MR. LEAR: "Here's something interesting.　I never
saw this man before, but I've met hundreds of his kind.
He is sharp and unscrupulous, easily imposes upon
people, and makes them think he's a sight better than
he is.　He is out of place here in this small town.　I
should naturally look for him in some big operation
at the West, where he would be carefully looking out
for Number One."

All of which shows that the detective was an excellent physiognomist.

MR. MAYHEW: "Who's this stranger, I wonder?
Don't look like a produce-buyer or a land-speculator.
I'd give half a dollar to know his business.　He's a
curious-looking man; he don't carry any marks that I
should know him by."

After breakfast the detective took a chair in the

hotel-office and smoked a cigar at leisure. Mr. Mayhew came out picking his teeth, threw a glance at the
stranger and went to his store.

"Who is that gentleman?" Mr. Lear asked of the
landlord.

"That is Weston Mayhew, our leading merchant
and the postmaster."

He examined the name of his guest on the register,
and remarked:

"You're a stranger here, I take it?"

"Years ago," was the reply, "I was in this part of
the country, but I never was in this village before."

"Buyer?" the landlord queried, with the off-hand
curiosity of a country host.   "Land or produce?"

"Neither."

"Hope I don't offend?"

"Oh, no," said Lear. "The fact is, I am out of a
job just now; I've retired from business, and become
what you might call a 'gentleman of elegant leisure.'
That's the best account I can give of myself."

"Oh!" said the landlord. He knew not what to say,
for this was something out of his experience.

"But I may tell you why I stopped at Bardwell."

The landlord listened eagerly.

"On one reason," added Mr. Lear, observing the
other's curiosity.

"My whole life has been passed at the West," he
went on, speaking slowly and thoughtfully; "that is,
the active part of it; all that makes *life* in this great,
stirring, hustling land of ours. I have been in large
affairs, and for thirty years have been on a continual
strain of mental and physical activity. I felt the need
of rest, and I concluded to take a long vacation; it
may become a permanent one. I am getting on in
years, landlord; the man who is near sixty has an uncertain hold on life. It occurred to me that the best use
I could make of my spare time would be to come East,
go up to Northern Vermont, to the old place where I

was born, and look up old friends and acquaintances. I am afraid I shall find few enough of them. Thirty years make a sad waste in any community. Still, I've got some of the old home-feeling left, and I'm going back there for a while."

"Where were you born and raised, sir?"

"In Dinsmore."

"Dinsmore? Seems to me some of our people here came from up that way."

"Yes; I happened to think of that as the train was getting in here, and I concluded to stop over and see if I could find any old friends. Can you mention any one that came from Dinsmore?"

"Let me see," said the landlord, thoughtfully. "There were the two Deans, but they are both dead. Wagner moved somewhere down South. I don't think of any one else but the Mulfords."

"I have heard that Lewis Mulford was dead."

"Yes, and his widow died most ten years ago."

Schooled as he was never to betray emotion, Elias Lear only concealed the effect that this announcement made upon him by hastily going to the door. Had he told the exact truth to the landlord, he would have told him that he had journeyed a thousand miles in the hope of finding the person whose death had just been announced to him, and that he had stopped at Bardwell to see her, and nobody else. And if the landlord could have seen the face that Mr. Lear turned to the street, he would have observed that a mist was gathering in those cold blue eyes.

"I have delayed too long," the detective sadly thought. "Well, *that* dream is over. I might as well turn westward again to-morrow and resume my old life."

When he came back and sat down again, there was no trace of his feelings in his face.

"You were speaking of Mrs. Jane Mulford," he

said. " I had not heard of her death. Tell me something of her and her husband."

"Well, sir, there's little to tell. A finer lady nor a better woman never lived, but I suppose her heart was broken by that gambling, horse-racing, hard-drinking scamp of a husband. The fellow had good looks, and that's the only good thing that he did have. He broke his neck on one of his sprees; 'twould have been a good thing for her if he'd done it before he ever saw her. Mrs. Mulford was poor enough; and Ernest was just getting so as to help her, when she died."

" Who is Ernest?"

" Her boy; only child; looks just like her; same handsome eyes and face."

" Is he in town now?"

" He was till a few weeks ago; and then, one morning, he turned up missing, and not a word has been heard of him. Beats the Jews, sir! — queerest thing I ever heard of. There's only one thing makes me think there isn't foul play somewhere about it."

The detective, without betraying it, was profoundly interested in the landlord's words.

" What is that?" he asked.

" Why, his employer has been giving out that Ernest has been stealing from the safe for a long time, and cleared out to save being arrested."

" Who was his employer?"

" Mr. Mayhew, the gentleman you saw at breakfast."

" Indeed! Is the story generally believed?"

" Well, I'm sorry to say that it is. It wouldn't be, about such an excellent young man as Ernest has always been — just like his mother, sir! — if anybody but Mr. Mayhew had told it. But he's the first man in the place; his word goes for anything."

" You say that nothing has been heard of this young man since he disappeared?"

"Not a word. His trunk is at his boarding-place; not a letter has come to anybody from him."

"Strange enough. Is there any other gossip about this affair?"

"A great deal, sir. The women folks say that Ernest was making up to June Gregory, the foster-daughter of his uncle and aunt. Mrs. Gregory and Mrs. Mulford were sisters. And they say that since he went away Mr. Mayhew himself has been paying a good deal of attention to pretty June."

"I think I will walk about the place awhile," Mr. Lear said.

As he went along the street he mused upon what the landlord had told him.

"If there isn't villainy somewhere in this," he soliloquized, "then the *detective instinct* in me is at fault. How naturally all these elements of a good case arrange themselves in the mind! Here is a young man in love with a pretty girl; his employer, almost old enough to be his father, falls in love with the same girl, and concocts a rascally plot to get the young man out of the way."

The words "detective instinct" were most appropriately applied by this man to himself. With the bare outline given him by the landlord, he had swiftly and unerringly reached the exact truth of the matter.

"And if I am right in my conjectures," he thought, "Jane Mulford's boy is being made the victim of a scoundrel. Because, if I read this Weston Mayhew's face rightly, he is capable of a great deal of crookedness."

He switched the weeds by the wayside with his stick, and kept on thinking.

"Well, I believe there *is* 'a divinity that shapes our ends.' Here I am, the whole object of my journey suddenly brought to nothing; poor Jane is long dead; any hope that I might have had of happiness with her, after the bitter disappointment of years past, has fled;

and a few moments since I was saying to myself that I would go back to the West at once, and resume the excitements and risks of my detective life. Then it is told to me that Jane's only child is under a cloud; that he has mysteriously disappeared; that insinuations of criminal conduct are flying about this community, where he has grown up from childhood with honor and respect; and the chatter of that inn-keeper leads me to suspect that Mr. Weston Mayhew's bad hand is in this business. Well, Elias Lear—what will you do about it? "

Thus he mused, as he walked along.

" I am nothing but a detective," he thought, with a smile. " Nature must have made me one, for I find it impossible to be anything else. Even on a vacation I am laying out work."

All this, unuttered, passed through his mind. Then came a thought that determined him.

" The landlord said that he looked like his mother. Poor, dear Jane! "

No one could have thought, in seeing this man, with his hard, dry aspect, and curt speech, that there had been romance in his life, and that there was now a soft spot in his heart. He took from the pocket within his vest a small miniature, opened the case, and gazed as he walked at the lovely face there portrayed.

" If she were alive," he mused, as he returned this memento of an unforgotten love to its place next his heart, " how eagerly, at her request, would I spring to the vindication of her son, and the clearing away of the web of villainy that I think has been woven around him. Does she not see him and me now? Is she not at this moment appealing to me to save her boy and punish his false accuser? "

He paused in his walk. The name of Weston Mayhew in large gilt letters over a door across the way attracted his attention. He slowly crossed the street.

Without any definite plan of operations in his mind he entered the store.

The resources of such men are simply wonderful. He wanted to see Mr. Mayhew and talk with him, hoping to get a clew that would aid him in unmasking the wrong that he was sure the merchant had committed. Yet he entered the store without any particular procedure outlined in his mind, trusting to the inspiration of the moment when he should be face to face with his man.

The door was open. He entered and noiselessly walked to the back part of the store. At first he thought that nobody else was there; but presently he saw Mr. Mayhew in his private office. His back was toward the detective; he was so profoundly interested in reading a letter that he did not hear the approach of the latter. He read the letter, and with his back still turned, tore letter and envelope to pieces and threw them into the waste basket.

CHAPTER XIII.

THE SILENT WITNESS.

THE detective, thus far unseen and unheard, stood directly behind Mr. Mayhew. He placed his hand on the shoulder of the merchant.

The latter started and whirled about. He trembled all over and there was a scared look in his face.

" Why, why," he stammered, " wh—wh—what d'ye want? "

" I beg your pardon, Mr. Mayhew," said the detective, with a smooth, bland voice well calculated to allay suspicion. " I wish to talk with you a few moments on a matter of business. Are you at leisure? "

" Yes," said the alarmed merchant, recovering himself. " You came in so sudden that you startled me. Pray be seated."

THE DETECTIVE PLACED HIS HAND UPON THE SHOULDER OF THE MERCHANT.—Page 75.

Hardly had Mr. Lear taken a chair when a lady entered the store and went to the postoffice window.

" Excuse me for a moment," said Mr. Mayhew. " I was compelled to discharge my clerk a while ago, and I have not succeeded in getting another to suit me. I will be back as soon as I wait on that lady."

The lady was June Gregory. She looked in her father's box, and saw that there was a letter there. Her heart beat faster; she hoped that it was for her, and from the person who was constantly in her thoughts.

The postoffice inclosure joined Mr. Mayhew's private office. The places were entirely distinct; you could not see from one into the other; and Mr. Lear, sitting in the private office, was out of sight of the postmaster behind the postoffice delivery-window. But the two places were so near together, that ordinary conversation carried on in one could be distinctly heard in the other.

The education of a professional detective teaches him to employ all his senses at once. Elias Lear had this faculty in a remarkable degree. He heard every word that passed between June and Mr. Mayhew; and his eyes made a remarkable discovery, his hands secured very valuable evidence.

" There is nothing for you, Miss Gregory," said Mayhew. " This letter is for your father."

He handed out the letter. And then, in a lower voice, but perfectly audible to Lear, he said.

" Will you be at home to-morrow night? "

" Yes."

" I shall do myself the pleasure of calling."

She made no reply. He came out from the postoffice, and accompanied her to the store-door.

" You looked and acted like a guilty man, Mr. Weston Mayhew," the detective thought, " when I surprised you, destroying that letter and envelope. If you do not furnish evidence against yourself, you will be different from most criminals in my experience."

His eyes sought the waste-basket. The fragments of the torn-up letter and envelope lay at the top of the waste-paper in it. From where he sat he saw that one small piece bore the letters, written in a large, round hand, " ulford."

The discovery was an inspiration to the detective. He turned one swift glance out into the store, to see that he was not observed. He was not; Mr. Mayhew had turned his back that way, as he walked to the door with June Gregory. Mr. Lear quickly gathered up the torn pieces of the letter and envelope, and thrust them into his pocket; when the merchant returned he was apparently absorbed in the perusal of a news-paper.

Mr. Mayhew came back to his office in good humor. He had just arranged with June to call on her the next evening; he had told her of his intention and she had not forbidden him to come. He had done all the talk-ing: she was silent and sad; but he had told her that he wanted to see her at home the following evening, and by her silence she had given consent. He knew that her foster-parents looked favorably on his suit; he smiled now, to think of the progress he was making.

"At this rate," he said to himself, "I shall marry her in a month. And then farewell forever to Bard-well."

He returned to his office. "Well, sir?" he said to the detective.

"I beg your pardon for troubling you on what you may think a trivial affair," said Mr. Lear, smoothly. "It is to me a matter of much consequence. I was passing your store, and I chanced to look up and see the name of *Mayhew*. When a young man I was in the Mexican war; I had a dear comrade of that name, who fell at Buena Vista. We were in Clay's Kentucky Riflemen. He often told me of a younger brother

whom he left at home. Never do I see the name of
Mayhew without inquiring for a relationship with my
dear old friend and comrade. Was he of kin to you?"

" No, sir; surely not. I had no brother and no rela-
tive in the Mexican war, that I know of."

" Ah! Pardon me, sir, for intruding."

" Don't mention it. Call again if you remain in
town."

" Thank you; I may remain here some weeks and
may drop in on you when you are at leisure."

" Good-morning, sir."

" Good-morning."

Mr. Weston Mayhew courteously bowed the gentleman out. Then he walked complacently the length
of his store half a dozen times. The faint chill, the
half suspicion that the guilty are apt to feel upon the
visit of a stranger, and which the merchant had distinctly
felt upon the appearance of Elias Lear, entirely van-
ished. He seemed to be a very harmless personage.

" I really hope that the soul of that unfortunate
Mayhew may rest in peace," chuckled the merchant to
himself, with a heavy attempt at a witticism.

Mr. Lear walked back to the hotel, calling at a book-
store on the way for a bottle of mucilage and some
sheets of stiff Bristol board. He went up to his room
with these, and locked the door. He took off his coat,
emptied the pocket of the fragments of paper and sat
down to the table.

The task of restoring a destroyed letter was a familiar one to him. He knew that it only required time
and patience.

In this case much time and much patience were required. There were at least fifty irregular pieces, some
as small as a ten-cent piece, and some torn with the
writing, so that the task of joining them was very diffi-
cult. As he progressed he discovered that at least three
pieces were missing. The places of these he supplied
with words, which he wrote in according to his idea of

what the original was, gathered from the restored parts.
When the whole was joined together, as children join
a puzzle-map, he read it over with mingled feelings of
satisfaction and indignation.

The envelope was postmarked at Granby, three days
before, and addressed to " Miss June Gregory, Bardwell."

The letter read as follows:

GRANBY, August 7, 1877.

DEAR JUNE — I almost despair of hearing from you.
Twice before have I written to you from here, and have
received no reply.

Let me repeat what I said to you in those letters.
Let me say it again.   Let me pray that you will not
be so cruel as to keep silence longer.

Dear June, I confess my fault.   I see now that I was
too headlong and rash with you.   I see now that you
were right.   You did not choose to be wooed in so
abrupt a way, and you resented it.   I do not blame
you.

But tell me to come back! Give me just a little hope
— if only a little — that you will some day love me.

I left Bardwell suddenly, after a kind of quarrel with
Mr. Mayhew.   I know not what he has said about me
since.   But I have done nothing wrong; I assure you
that I have not.   Do not you, June, believe an ill word
of me.

Most faithfully yours,
ERNEST MULFORD.

The detective locked up the restored letter in his
satchel.

" You are just like the common run of criminals, Mr.
Mayhew," he said to himself.   " You will furnish me
all the evidence against you that I need.   All you need
is close and skillful watching.   And that waste-basket
of yours is a treasure-house of information.   I must
manage to get hold of it."

CHAPTER XIV.

THE DETECTIVE AT WORK.

THE skillful manipulations by which the detective obtained possession of the merchant's waste-paper basket late one night and returned it early in the morning, need not be particularly set forth. The coveted prize was obtained by bribing the man who was entrusted with a key over night, in order to sweep out the store and set it to rights. If the means that Mr. Lear found necessary to employ in order to obtain full and sufficient evidence of the merchant's crime were not such as all people would commend, it is, nevertheless, true that they were such as he was accustomed to employ, and by aid of which he had been remarkably successful. And he felt perfectly justified in his course, it being with him a favorite saying, " When you fight the Devil, you must use his own weapons."

But it must not be supposed that this task was easily or quickly accomplished. The detective had to move slowly and cautiously, and he did not dare take any risk by which Mr. Mayhew's suspicions might be aroused. In roundabout ways he discovered who it was that took care of the store; at what hours of the night he was engaged in his task; next, that this man secretly disliked Mr. Mayhew for what he called his " blamed stinginess to me." The man was poor; and while he would not permit the store to be robbed through his connivance, he saw no harm in letting " the gentleman at the tavern " take the useless waste-paper for a few hours, especially since he paid him fifty dollars for his agency in the matter. Nor did it trouble Jim Blynn's conscience that he was required to make a solemn promise never to divulge this transaction.

The basket was stealthily delivered to Mr. Lear at the back door of the store, concealed in a large sack;

A Sharp Night's Work 6

by him it was conveyed to his room at the hotel, where, with locked door, the detective was employed for four hours in scrutinizing every piece of paper in the whole bushel.   Each morsel that bore writing like that upon Ernest Mulford's restored letter, already in his possession, was carefully laid aside, and also numerous pieces which bore a delicate female hand.   This task performed, and the multitude of precious fragments locked in a drawer, the basket and its remaining worthless contents were cautiously returned to Blynn.

But something further was necessary, Mr. Lear thought, to prevent any suspicion from lingering in the merchant's mind.   Supposing that it should happen to occur to Mayhew that the waste-basket was an unsafe place for the numerous letters that he had stolen and destroyed, even in their fragmentary condition—supposing that he should make a search and fail to find a single piece, would he not be alarmed, and perhaps evade justice by flight?   Thinking of this possibility, Jim Blynn was directed by the detective to empty out the contents of the basket and burn them.

The empty basket quickly attracted Mayhew's attention that morning.   He called Blynn, and inquired what he knew about it.

" I threw out the old paper and burnt it, sir," was the answer.   " The basket was gettin' full."

" Who told you to do that? "

" Nobody, sir."

" After this, you wait for orders before destroying anything about here.   Are you sure you burned *all* the waste paper there? "

" Every bit of it, sir," lied Jim, promptly.

" Show me where you burned it."

The merchant followed his man out in rear of the store, and saw a black spot on the ground, with a little heap of gray ashes and embers.

He was perfectly satisfied!

"I ought to have burned those scraps myself," he muttered. "No matter; it is all right now."

So much time had the detective found it necessary to occupy with the business of securing the torn-up letters and envelopes, that it was now the third of September. As everybody in a place like Bardwell inquires about everybody else's affairs, the continued stay of Mr. Lear at the hotel naturally occasioned some comment. He found it convenient and safe to continue to bear the character which he had appeared in to the landlord: a gentleman of leisure from the West, passing a vacation at ease, and remaining at Bardwell because he found it a pleasant place. He made some acquaintances, and by strolling and idling about perfectly sustained that character. He overcame his repugnance to Weston Mayhew sufficiently to have an occasional talk with him about indifferent things, and surprised the merchant by exhibiting much ignorance about business in general.

"The fellow is a greenhorn," said Mayhew to himself. "He don't look like it, but his talk plainly shows it."

Almost another week was occupied by the detective in the secrecy of his room in sorting out the torn fragments, and putting them properly together. It was emphatically a work of skill and patience; but he finally had the satisfaction of reading in their restored condition all the letters that Ernest had written to June and others from Granby, as well as the one letter mailed by her to him. Here was overwhelming proof upon which Weston Mayhew could be convicted in a District Court of robbing the mails, and sent to the penitentiary. The sole piece of this kind of his rascality that was not known at this time, and which did not transpire till after some stirring events yet to be recounted had happened, was the forgery that he had mailed to June in the name of Ernest Mulford, unsuspected by her.

With the evidence now in his possession, Mr. Lear sat down and seriously thought of what his next step should be.

Should he make a complaint, and have Mayhew promptly arrested?

Not yet. Ernest Mulford was a necessary witness; he must first go to Granby and secure him.

Should he not go at once?

He thought he should not be ready for some days yet. Ernest's last letter from the waste-basket was only a little more than a week old; he did not think there was immediate danger of his leaving there.

The detective in his casual talks with the landlord and others had secured the gossip of the village as to the merchant's wooing. It was reported that he visited at Mr. Gregory's as often as two evenings in the week. There could be no doubt that he was courting June.

But there was something in Mr. Mayhew's conduct that Lear had not yet fathomed, and something that puzzled him. He observed that on at least three different nights the merchant was absent from the hotel, returning before breakfast. What did this mean? He must find out.

He did find out; and a pretty discovery it was!

———

CHAPTER XV.

SHADOWED BY NIGHT.

ELEVEN O'CLOCK at night of September 14th. The detective was on the watch, as he had been for the last three nights. Upon each of those nights he knew that Weston Mayhew had retired to his room in the hotel about ten o'clock.

But on this night the merchant went back to the store after supper. At eleven o'clock he was still there. The detective, lingering among the shadows of the great trees opposite, remained out of sight himself, but kept a close watch upon the store-door.

"If he stays in there all night," he reflected, "this kind of thing will never do. I shall never find out what deviltry he is up to."

The store-door at this instant was cautiously opened, and Mr. Mayhew appeared. He locked the door, looked carefully up and down the street, saw no one, and then swiftly walked down a cross-street near by.

He went some distance on this street, and turned down another. He met but two or three persons, and was always careful to cross to the opposite side before the one approaching was near enough to recognize him. Skulking along in this way, in about twenty minutes he had reached a cosy-looking cottage at the southern outskirts of the village.

He paused in front of it, and looked all about. Within a stone's throw of where he stood Elias Lear was concealed behind the trunk of a great elm — and very safely concealed.

The detective saw Mr. Mayhew take up a few pebbles from the walk, and throw them against the window.

The house had been quite dark, but upon this signal a light appeared at a window.

The front door was opened in such a way as not to disclose who was within. Mr. Mayhew quickly entered; the door was closed again and locked.

The light reappeared, but now at the windows on the side of the house. The light was soft, as if from a lamp turned down.

Along this side ran a verandah, with steps at the end. Two windows came down to within eighteen inches of the floor of the verandah. Both were shuttered; one was slightly raised, the night being warm. The curtain was half raised.

At one glance the detective took in all these details. He saw by the way the light came through the slats of the shutters that the curtain must be somewhat raised. He had quickly removed his shoes, and creeping stealthily along the verandah, lay at full length under the window. He heard a murmur of voices within, which told him that the window was a little raised.

Perfectly concealed in the shadow where he lay, he could not have been discovered from the street, or even from within the window, except by aid of a lamp.

Something more than voices he heard. The sound of kissing, twice repeated, came plainly to his ear.

His position was painful, but he dared not take the risk yet of sitting upright. Instead, he elevated his shoulders so that his ear was on the level of the lower part of the blind.

Then, not only voices, but words were plainly heard. He listened, and drank in every syllable.

" O Weston, I'm so glad to see you again! " The voice was that of a woman, soft and musical, but rather loud.

" Well, Phebe," Mr. Mayhew replied, " I'll believe it, even if you don't let all the neighbors know it."

" Forgive me, Weston; I'll speak lower. I always feel so happy when you come, that I forget to be prudent. Let me kiss you again."

A significant sound indicated that she had done as she wished.

" Well, how is everything to-night? Are we safe?"

" O, yes; I got everything ready when you let me know that you were coming."

" Where's that domestic?"

" I let her go home till to-morrow. She won't be back till seven."

" And there's nobody about to look in on us, or overhear what we say?"

" No, Weston; not a soul. Make yourself easy about that."

" Has anything happened since I was here to make you think anybody suspects us?"

"Not a thing.   I believe our secret is perfectly safe."

"Very good.   Because if I had any reason to think that I had been seen or known to come here, I can tell you of a certain lady who would leave Bardwell immediately."

A suppressed cry came from the woman.

"O Weston, dear Weston, you would not send me away?"

"Indeed I would, Phebe; indeed I will, whenever I discover that there is the least whisper about you and me."

"You are so cruel!   I don't believe you love me."

"Now, Phebe, don't be foolish!   I love you enough to satisfy any reasonable woman, and I will continue to just so long as it is safe.   But I tell you now, as I have told you before, that our love must be in secret. Let any living person know of it, and I'll send you off without the slightest compunction."

A sound of sobbing reached the ear of the detective. The conversation was suspended while it continued; but he heard the sound of Mr. Mayhew's feet as he walked to and fro in the room.

An overpowering desire to see the two, as well as to hear them, seized upon him.   They were now absorbed in themselves, and in the subject of their talk, so that the attempt could be safely made.   Mr. Lear raised his eyes to the shutter, and looked through the slats.

CHAPTER XVI.

THE WOMAN IN THE CASE.

HE saw Weston Mayhew pacing up and down the room, biting his nails, and frowning.

The apartment was elegantly furnished and carpeted. Ornaments and bric-a-brac in profusion were there. An upright piano stood in the corner.   Beautiful oil paint-

ings decorated the walls. Everything that money and
taste could do to make a charming bower of this room,
had been done. A glimpse was had through an open
door of a luxuriously furnished bed-chamber. A gas
chandelier, hanging from the ceiling, was brilliant with
pendants; but the light was turned down.

A large, but perfectly proportioned woman, of about
thirty years, sat in one of the deep easy chairs. She
was drying her eyes with a lace handkerchief, and the
concealed watcher at once recognized her as a lady who
had been pointed out on the street to him as Mrs.
Phebe Bashford, a wealthy widow. She wore a rich
dress of blue silk, low in the neck and with short
sleeves, which harmonized with her dark beauty. She
had great masses of hair that was almost black, arranged
in coils upon her head, large dark eyes, regular and
handsome features. To men easily impressed by
female beauty, her smile was enchanting. Diamonds
glittered in her ears and upon her fingers.

Weston Mayhew passed in his walk near her. She
rose and threw her arms about his neck. He did not
repulse her; he stood there rather indifferently, while
the magnificent creature, overrunning with love and
emotion, clasped him in her arms, and laid her head on
his shoulder.

"Do forgive me, Weston," she pleaded. "I
know I vex you by my importunities, but I can't help
it. I want you all the time; I want you all to myself."

He sat down in the chair that she had just vacated.
She threw herself on an ottoman at his feet, resting her
white arms on his knees, and looking pleadingly up
into his face.

"Then behave yourself," he said. "Be reasonable.
Take what you can get of me, and be thankful for it.
You ought to be glad that I don't repudiate you alto-
gether."

Her bosom heaved convulsively; her eyelids shook
with quick-springing tears.

" Now, see here, Phebe," said Mr. Mayhew, pettishly,
" you are putting in rather more of the doleful to-night
than I can stand.   What is it that you complain of?"

" I don't complain, Weston; I won't."

" But you do whenever I come here.   You know
that I come to enjoy myself with you, and I hate
these tears and wailings.   Haven't you got everything
here you want? — books, fine furniture, music, a servant
to wait on you?"

" Yes, Weston; but ——"

" Don't I give you money enough?   Here is some
now."

He drew a wad of bank-notes from his vest pocket
and threw it into her corsage.

" You are too generous with me, Weston.   I don't
need ——"

" And you have diamonds, haven't you? — and fine
dresses?"

" Yes; but ——"

" Don't the ladies call on you?   Are you not petted,
and flattered, and invited out to parties and teas because you are supposed to be Mrs. Phebe Bashford, the
rich California widow? "

She assented by her silence.

" Some of the men are making sheep's-eyes at you,
ain't they?   It wouldn't be a bad idea, Phebe, if you
find one you like, and rich enough to relieve me of any
further responsibility, to marry him."

Her dark eyes flashed.

" Weston Mayhew! " she cried, indignantly.

" Oh, suit yourself, Phebe; I don't care.   I find it
pleasant enough to pass some hours with you in secret
every week, when you won't go into your heroics.
What do you want? — tell me frankly."

" I will.   I don't like this stolen love.   There is a
sting to it; it leaves a sorrow behind."

" Now you're getting poetical and romantic, Phebe.

I tell you, the only kind of love that can exist between you and me is just this kind.   So make the best of it."

She shuddered, but went on, with an effort:

" I meet you on the street, and I have to bow politely to you, as I would to any one else.   I meet you at parties, and you have formal compliments for me, just the same as for any other woman.   Nobody dreams that I have a better right to you than any other woman can have.   The other night at Mrs. Hamlin's party you took that pert minx, June Gregory, out to supper, and waited on her home after the party was over.   How do you suppose it made *me* feel to see such things? "

" I don't know, Phebe.   I almost said, ' I don't care.'   And I don't — much.   I repeat what I said before, you had better make the best of it, be reasonable, and enjoy what you can get out of me."

Mr. Mayhew stuck out his legs, and yawned.

" I want more than you give me."

" Indeed!   Well, tell me what you want, that you haven't got."

Her reply came as distinctly to the ear of the detective at the shutter as had the previous conversation.

" I want you to take me home to you, and acknowledge me to the world for what I am — your lawful wife!"

He heard, and he thrust her violently from him. She clasped her hands and looked beseechingly into his face.

" Oh, that's your game, is it, Mrs. Bashford? " he said.   " My wife, are you?   How would you go to work to prove it?"

" We were lawfully married," she sobbed.

" Grant it.   In California, more than ten years ago, by a magistrate.   You've told me a dozen times that you never got a certificate."

She was silent.

" Is that true? "

" I have told you so."

" I say, *is it true?* "

" Yes," she answered, with her face turned from him.

" Pretty fix you'd be in, then!" he scornfully said. " Claim to be married to Weston Mayhew, indeed!— the biggest man in Bardwell. No certificate to prove it. If the witnesses are living, which is doubtful, they are three thousand miles away; upon my indignant denial, you'd be warned out of town, as an adventuress."

" O, nothing could exceed your cruelty! Why did I not die, instead of following you here? "

" I sometimes think that it *would* have been in better taste," the man brutally replied. " But say we *were* married. You know that you consented to keep it secret in California; and you know why. *You* did the wooing, madam; you were love-crazy after me. I was quite indifferent to the whole business. I consented to a marriage, to save your scruples; but only on condition that the thing should be kept perfectly dark. Well, we lived there at Yerba Buena about as we have lived here. When I got ready to come East, I made an ample provision there for you and your boy, and bade you good-by, hoping and expecting never to see you again. But, two years ago, you came to Bardwell."

" I could not help it," the unhappy woman pleaded, amid her fast-falling tears. " My darling boy died, my precious West! O, how like you he looked and acted! and I could not stay there alone. I was hungering for love; I wanted *you*. I came here; you know I have obeyed you; you know how closely the secret has been guarded, and you know how grateful I have been for all that you have done for me. But I want — Oh, how I crave to have you publicly acknowledge me as your wife."

" Well, then, madam, we might as well have a plain understanding as not.   I never will."

" Never?"

" No, never!"

She did not faint, nor shriek, nor plead. She looked at him in an apathy of despair.

" You will kill me," she said.   " But I love you well enough yet to die for you."

" You needn't die yet awhile," was his answer. " Phebe, I wasn't joking a minute ago, when I said that the correct thing would be for you to get married. You see ——"

She gave a fierce little cry, such as a wounded lioness might utter.

" Oh, well, it's all one to me.   I only mention it, because the time is coming when such an arrangement would probably be more comfortable to you.   The fact is, I am very likely to be married myself before long."

Her eyes, her whole face, were eloquent with rage and passion.

" What!" she cried.   " To June Gregory?"

" Yes; you might as well know."

" You won't dare do it!"

"Indeed I will, my dear.   *You* are certainly in no condition to prevent it."

" I'll kill her! "

He laughed in her face.

" I'll kill myself! " she cried, with a flood of tears.

Weston Mayhew put an arm about the waist of the enraged, sobbing woman, and raised her up.   He took her handkerchief and wiped her eyes; he smoothed her tumbled hair; he even called her " Queen Phebe," the pet name he had given her of old, and once he kissed her lips.   She was won back to gentle words by his tenderness; she smiled through her tears, and put a well-rounded arm about his neck.

Let us pity her; let us not condemn her.   There

is no more sorrowful spectacle in the world than that of the woman who loves too well.

Learning every word of this strange interview, the detective knew that something of the highest importance was yet to come.

———

CHAPTER XVII.

UNDER THE SPELL.

A CLEAR chime from the ormolu clock on the marble shelf had some time before marked the hour of midnight.

" Are you tired, dear Weston?" the woman asked.

" Yes; and, to tell the whole truth, devilish hungry, too."

" I'm glad to hear you say that," she said, clapping her hands gleefully. " I thought I should please you, Weston. I had Emilia cook a chicken and make some biscuit for you. Wait a very few minutes while I go and set the table, and make a cup of tea."

She left the room. The detective saw the merchant take two or three hasty turns about the room. An aggravating hint had arisen out of the conversation just had, and Mr. Mayhew was tormented by it to that extent that he began to soliloquize about it.

" I wonder if the jade really has a marriage certificate?"

The concealed listener had noted the hesitation with which the woman denied having such a paper. And he had observed the suspicion that at the instant showed itself in Mayhew's face.

" It is just like a woman to get such a thing secretly, keep it quietly and lie about it when asked. I'd give one thousand dollars this moment to be certain about it."

Another turn about the room and the merchant muttered an expression of satisfaction.

" That's it — that's it!   By the Lord Harry, I'll make her tell."

The woman appeared in the doorway at this moment, smiling and holding out her jeweled white hand.

" Come, Weston," she said.   " All ready."

" Wait a moment, Phebe," Mr. Mayhew exclaimed. " There's something important I forgot to tell you. Sit down here in this chair — that's it.   Do you remember the view from the windows of your sitting-room in the California home — the view of the distant mountain peaks, with their tops covered with snow, and the beautiful effect of sunrise and sunset upon them, and ——"

He was sitting directly before her, looking steadily into her eyes, talking straight on, without break or pause.   She seemed uneasy just after he had begun, and struggled as if to rise from the chair.   She could not.   All her faculties were under the control of the man before her, who was exerting over her his mesmeric powers, to which she was susceptible in a remarkable degree.   A few passes before her face with his hands completed the mysterious spell — a spell the nature of which science cannot yet define.   She sighed, slightly yawned, her eyes closed, and she was in a perfect mesmeric trance.   Weston Mayhew smiled; he knew he could direct her thoughts and speech into any channel that he chose.

" You said you were married," he pronounced in a low but distinct voice.   He took her hands, so that the influence might be more positive.

" Yes, I was," the sleeper uttered.

" But you had no certificate?"

" I did.   I went to the magistrate one day and got it; and he got the witnesses to sign it.   Weston did not know it, but I got it."

" You have not got it now? "

" I have got it now."

" Where is it? "

She struggled in her sleep; she spoke through her shut teeth.

" I never told where it is kept.   That is my secret."

" Where is it? " was repeated in the same cold, calm voice.

She hesitated again.   Her face worked.   She did not answer.

" *Where — is — the — marriage — certificate?* "

The answer came reluctantly, but quite distinct:

" In Shakespeare's Plays, at the beginning of Timon of Athens. "

Mr. Mayhew walked over to a bookcase with glass doors, selected the volume, opened it to the place indicated, and there found the paper.   He carefully examined it; then, to the surprise of the watcher, instead of putting it in his pocket, he shut it up again in the book.

But his meaning quickly occurred to the detective. Should he then abstract it, Mrs. Bashford (as we will still call her) might discover its loss, and be led to do something desperate.   He could secure it any time, now that he knew where it was, and he would wait until the last visit he proposed to make to this house, immediately before his marriage with June Gregory, and then secure and destroy the obnoxious paper.

So Mr. Mayhew reasoned, and so the detective interpreted his forbearance on the spot.

The merchant came back to the subject in the chair, still held in the chains of her trance, and, with a few passes with his hands about her face, set her free.   She opened her eyes, stared around her, and seemed bewildered.

" Why, what has happened? " she cried.   " What am I sitting down here for? "

" I said that I was tired as well as hungry, when you asked me," replied Mayhew, coolly.   " But I did not suppose *you* were going to sit down right here after calling me to supper, and go to sleep."

Her laughter rang a clear, merry peal through the room.

"Did I really do that? Why, what got into me? I didn't know I was sleepy; don't believe I was. It's very stupid of me. But come out to tea, and don't say anything more about it."

The hypocrite placed his arm about her, simulating an affection that might deceive her. How willing she was to be deceived! She placed her clasped hands on his shoulder and reached up for a kiss, murmuring the words:

"Be good to me, Weston; Oh, do be good to me!"

The detective's fingers were passed through between the slats of the blinds; the blind was unhasped, the window raised, and he stepped lightly into the vacant room. In not more than one minute he had secured the certificate from the volume, and was out again on the verandah, re-closing the window and the blinds. He walked to the steps and put on his shoes. He was stiff and aching from the constraint of the position he had kept so long; but he was filled with the sense of his triumph.

"I hope Madam will not look for that paper before I confront Mr. Weston Mayhew with it," he reflected. "If she should, it can't be helped; she shall have justice, any way."

Not until he had gained his room at the hotel, locked the door, and lit the gas, did he examine his prize. It read thus:

State of California, } ss. Be it remembered, that County of Mendocino, } on this 9th day of November, A. D. 1865, at Yerba Buena, I, the undersigned, a magistrate of said county, have joined in the estate of matrimony, according to the laws of said State, Weston Mayhew, merchant, aged 36, and Phebe Bashford, spinster, aged 20. CARLOS NOGALES.

Witnesses: PETER BLUNT, ALONZO CANALIS.

" You are fast getting to the end of your tether, Mr. Mayhew," he said, as he put away the certificate.

The detective went to bed, but the exciting events of the night kept him awake. When he did at last fall asleep, his slumber was light. In the hour next before daylight he was drowsing, rather than sleeping. He heard footfalls outside. They passed his door and went on along the hall. He rose, unclosed his door without noise, and listened. The second door from his on the other side was opened and closed. It was Weston Mayhew's room. Like a thief in the night he had skulked back from Mrs. Bashford's just before the dawn.

" I have sometimes pitied the men that I have delivered to justice," mused the detective. " But there will be no pity for you, you cold-blooded scoundrel! "

CHAPTER XVIII.

PERVERSE FATES.

THE three days next following were days of deep thought and anxiety to Elias Lear.

He was — or he thought he was — master of the situation. But his course was not exactly clear to him.

The whole experience and history of his detective life had been one repeated lesson against precipitation. He had learned not to frighten away the bird before it was fairly in the net.

He was strongly tempted to go straight to Emmanuel Gregory, although a stranger to him, and, exhibiting the marriage certificate, convict Weston Mayhew of intended bigamy, and expose him to the scorn and detestation of the whole village.

We know now that had he done so June would have been instantly rescued from the clutch of this human hyena, and the stirring events of the night of September 18th, yet to be detailed at length, would have been averted.

But the one fatal item of information that the detective did not obtain, and which it was hardly possible for him to obtain in advance, was, that the wedding was to take place on that evening.

In fact, the invitations were never issued till the evening of the 17th. Mr. Mayhew had grown suspicious and anxious about Mrs. Bashford. The incident of the certificate had alarmed him. Another incident still more alarmed him. He had set in his own mind the night of the 16th as the time that he would make a last visit to that house, and by stealth and stratagem obtain the certificate. He went, as usual, in the dead of night; he threw gravel against the window, but his signal was not answered. The house continued dark. He ventured to try the door, but it was locked. He went away in a most unpleasant frame of mind.

What did it mean? Was Mrs. Bashford sulky, and so unmindful of his signal? Or had she gone away somewhere, on some mission of mischief to himself?

Whichever it was, he resolved that his wedding should take place quickly, and with as little notice as possible. By what lies he satisfied June and her parents that there was need of great haste, as well as secrecy, need not be related. The preparations went on, quietly and prosperously; the Gregorys proud and delighted that June should wed the foremost man of the village, the more easily overlooked the strangeness of his anxiety for dispatch and silence as to an event which is commonly ushered in with joy and publicity.

Mr. Mayhew had also a lurking uneasiness in regard to his crimes against the mails. He began to dread the sudden reappearance of Ernest Mulford in the village. He began to say to himself that he was running serious risks, and that he had better put an end to them.

He was venturing everything in his headstrong passion for June. And, as Mr. Lear afterward shrewdly guessed, he had made his arrangements not to return to Bardwell. He had quietly turned his property into money, or easily handled securities; even his store he had sold by correspondence to parties in New York, who knew him and the stock, and who bought upon the inventory furnished, to be delivered on the 19th. He had forwarded his resignation as postmaster. And poor June! She little thought, her blind and deluded parents never imagined, that she was being sold to a modern Bluebeard, who was proposing for her and for himself an exile of thousands of miles, from which there would be no return!

Thus it will easily be seen how the detective, with the whole community, was misled in regard to the time of the wedding. When Mr. Lear was saying to himself that there was plenty of time yet for him to publish the marriage certificate to all Bardwell, the wedding that was to make Weston Mayhew a bigamist, and June Gregory a forlorn, deceived bride, was on the eve of being celebrated.

But on the morning of the 18th Mr. Lear determined that the time was ripe for his own thunderbolt to be hurled at the guilty man, and for Ernest Mulford's vindication.

He resolved to go to Granby, without letting his mission or his whereabouts be known. He would find Ernest; he would have affidavits drawn up, and warrants obtained; they would return with a marshal, and Mr. Mayhew would be arrested on so many separate charges that it would not be possible for him to obtain bail. He would be jailed, convicted in due time, and consigned to the penitentiary. Ernest's vindication would follow, as a matter of course; explanations between him and June could not fail to make them lovers; and Mrs. Bashford's true story should be made public — although he rather expected that the infatuated woman would break her heart over her graceless husband in a felon's cell.

All this the detective planned as he took the cars at Bardwell for Granby on the morning of the 18th. " Man proposes — God disposes." We have seen the untoward result. The astounding discovery that the wedding at Mr. Gregory's was to take place that very night; the breathless race against time; the maddening failure, when casualty had been piled upon casualty, and fate, time and accident all seemed aiding the wicked and overwhelming the innocent — these things have been sufficiently related. At half-past nine o'clock of that night the contest was apparently over; the fight was lost! The detective lay sick at the little inn at Granby; Ernest Mulford, weary, beaten, fainting, was making his revelation to his relatives and their guests, horror stricken at the mansion, and the triumphant bigamist and his cruelly deceived bride were speeding westward from Bardwell on their wedding journey, from which Weston Mayhew expected that there would be no return!

But the night was not yet gone.

CHAPTER XIX.

THE TELEGRAM.

DISTRESS, agitation, curiosity pervaded the Gregory mansion. With the startling arrival of Ernest Mulford, and with the tidings that he bore, all the joyous festivities were instantly suspended. A very painful awkwardness began to prevail among the guests. Either a great woe or a great fright and scandal were impending over this family, and at this most inopportune of all hours. The guests sadly began to realize that they were in the way. By twos and threes they got ready and took their departure, most of them refraining from bidding the host and hostess good-night.

Poor Mrs. Gregory sat rocking to and fro and wringing her hands, moaning, " O June!—O my dear lost June!" Mr. Gregory stood in perfect bewilderment, hardly able to comprehend the full force of the blow. A few intimate friends had remained; some of the ladies were endeavoring to soothe Mrs. Gregory, and three or four of the men-folk were standing about, anxious to do something, but at a loss what to do.

Ernest Mulford's overstrained system seemed to have given way. The fiery energy that had thus far borne him up had halted beneath the shock of failure; and when the will faltered, nerves and muscles gave way. He sat listlessly, his eyes fixed on the floor, paying no heed to any one present.

At this juncture Dr. Eldridge stepped forward. The doctor was a sleek, rotund person, fond of society and good cheer, but well skilled in his profession.

" This is most extraordinary, Mr. Mulford," he said. " Have you proof of what you say? "

" Full proof," said Ernest, in a voice hardly above a whisper.

" Is it not possible that you wrongly accuse Mr. Mayhew of having a living wife before the marriage of to-night? "

" The certificate of his marriage to Mrs. Phebe Bashford is in my pocket. She will corroborate it."

" O the villain! " Mrs. Gregory moaned. " Right here among us, and he kept it secret, so he could destroy our precious June forever. Now I see why he insisted on being so hasty and so quiet about the wedding."

" It is extremely awkward and distressing," the doctor said. " And I'm afraid we can do nothing at present. Mr. Mayhew and his bride are now well on their way to New York. I don't see how he can be apprehended. We will have to wait till they return. It will be a dreadful thing for any one to break the news

to June; but she will have to know it then, when her
— when Mr. Mayhew is arrested."

Ernest opened his heavy eyes and looked up.

" If we wait till that scoundrel appears again in
Bardwell before we arrest him," he said, " we shall
wait a long time.   None of us will ever see him here
again.   Aunt Jerusha, you will never see June again
if he is not overtaken.   He will go to the ends of the
earth with her."

There was a fresh burst of sobbing from Mrs.
Gregory.

" O, Emmanuel, Ernest, can't you overtake them?"

" The villain has made every preparation for this
flight," the young man went on.   " He has sold his business here to New York people, who will be here to-
morrow to take charge of it.   He has converted all his
large property into cash and securities, which I doubt
not he has on his person and in his trunk."

" Can't we telegraph to arrest him?" Mr. Gregory
asked.   " I am willing to do anything to reach the
monster and to secure our poor child.   It is a judgment
upon me, for my eagerness to get wealth and position
for June, and for believing such shocking lies of you,
Ernest."   And the speaker groaned in his distress.

" Don't reproach yourself, uncle; almost everybody
has been deceived and blinded with you.   Yes, we
can and will do something yet!   I am bruised in body
and tortured in mind; had I arrived here in time to
get the clutches of the law on the man whom you
justly call a monster, to save June and satisfy her that I
have been foully wronged, and that she and I have been
separated through the machinations of scheming villainy — had I come in time for all this, I say, I should
now be abed, with the doctor here attending to me.
As it is, I must go on; I will not falter in this pursuit
till I succeed — or till I perish!   Weak and sick as I
am, I have a plan already formed in my mind; if there

had been the losing of any time in it by talking with you here, I should not have delayed here a minute."

He tottered to the sofa, threw himself down, and continued to talk.

" I must try to rest a little, while I tell you what is to be done. Doctor, get a time-table; see if this train that has just left with Weston Mayhew and June stops at Randolph."

" I have a table in my pocket-book," was the answer Yes, here it is; Randolph, 10:10."

" And at Beaverton? "

" Beaverton, 11:30," read the doctor.

" That will do, Doctor; write a telegram with all speed to the station-police at Randolph, to arrest Mayhew. Make it full enough, and strong enough, and sign uncle's name to it."

Some of Ernest's spirit had infused itself into those about him.

" Yes, and I'll take it right over to the office," eagerly said Mr. Gregory. " There's a horse and buggy all ready in the barn, that I had hitched up to do errands to-night. Doctor Eldridge lends it."

The doctor produced a blank from his capacious pocket-book, and wrote the dispatch. Ernest was dozing, but the loud tones of the doctor, as he read what he had written, aroused him.

" Take it over, uncle, and see that the operator puts it right through. What's the time?"

" Twenty minutes to ten."

" There's half an hour, then. But make haste, and wait for an answer. Come back at once when you get it."

Mr. Gregory hurried away.

" I hope it'll do the business," said the doctor. " But whether it does or no, you've got to go to bed at once, Mr. Mulford. You are feverish; where's your pulse?"

" No bed for me to-night, Dr. Eldridge."

" But you've got to rest, you must have sleep."

" I'm going to get the dust brushed off from me, and have some cold water on my head. Aunty, get me some kind of a coat to put on in place of this, that is almost ripped off of me. And please make me some coffee, hot and strong; I shall want it when I wake up."

" You won't wake up till daylight," said the doctor.

" I can tell you one thing: I won't go to sleep unless you promise, on your honor, that you will wake me up the moment my uncle comes back."

" Well, I promise," said the doctor, seeing that opposition was useless.

After his ablution and the use of the brush, with some changes in his torn garments, Ernest lay down again and was instantly lost in sleep. He was awakened by the doctor, in forty minutes, and he heard his uncle groan:·

" It's no use. We can't stop them! "

CHAPTER XX.

AFTER THE MARRIAGE.

THE ceremony had been performed at the Gregory mansion; the vows interchanged that bound the man of forty-eight to the maiden of nineteen, for life; the congratulations had been spoken, the collation disposed of, amid light, laughter and flowers; and as the time grew pressing the farewells were said, the elaborate toilets of the bride and groom were exchanged for traveling costumes, and Mr. Weston and June entered the carriage that was to carry them to the station. There was a chorus of God-speeds, a shower of rice, and a volley of old shoes sent after the couple; and then the two were alone together.

The first moment when the newly-married couple are alone!— it is a serious one.

When the minister had pronounced the two man and wife, and congratulated them, the groom saluted the unresisting lips of his bride.

Now, in the solitude of the carriage, on that short ride to the station, he took her hand, he put his arm about her waist, and sought to draw her to him. He breathed in her ear the impassioned words, " My darling wife."

She turned her face from him; she would not permit him to kiss her lips again. He had to be content with pressing his to her cheek.

He heard the sound of her sobbing; he felt the convulsive throbbing of her form. And he leaned back in the cushions of the carriage, and was supremely content. " It is," he thought, " but the natural aud usual exhibition of maiden modesty. She is also grieved at leaving her home and friends for the first time. Patience, Weston Mayhew! You have fairly won the prize; treat her tenderly now, and she will soon and gladly come to your arms."

So he thought; and until the carriage drove up to the Bardwell station his arm remained around her, and more than once he whispered, " My darling wife!"

She did not turn her head, nor yield to his caresses or endearing words. What spell possessed her? What were her thoughts in that hour?

She had wedded the richest and the foremost man in Bardwell. She had become the envy of the unmarried part of its women; she had satisfied the ambition of her simple foster parents; she had thought to satisfy herself.

Had she done it?

Alas! now, in the first hour of her wifehood, when the glare and glitter, the music and the excitement of the evening were things of the past, and she was brought sternly face to face with the man whom she had but just vowed to love, honor and cherish till death did them part—she bitterly confessed to herself that she did *not* love him, never had loved him, and never could.

The story of her wooing and winning was simple enough, and might well be imagined from what has been told.   She had been, as she thought, rudely repulsed in her effort to be reconciled to Ernest Mulford.   The seeming repulse had bitterly humiliated her, as it would have humiliated any woman.   Her pride was wounded; and when, just at that time, Mr. Mulford made his first advances, she was in the mood to encourage them, and thus to show Ernest Mulford and all others that her affections need not go begging. For Weston Mayhew personally she had never entertained the very first spark of genuine affection.   Indeed, how could it be, that this young, lovely, winsome creature, could love this gross and sensual being, with all his years, and even with his riches?   She was overcome by wounded pride, by the appeals of her parents, by the perseverance of the suitor, with the golden prizes that he held out to her.   With Ernest Mulford forgotten, or remembered only to be revenged upon, she was in that condition described by the poet:

> " Women, like moths, are ever caught by glare,
> And Mammon wins his way where seraphs might despair. "

They descended from the carriage, in the glare of the station lamps.   She took his offered arm and accompanied him to the waiting-room.   Her face was white and fixed.   It would have been awful to see for any person who well knew her — the rigid, hopeless face of that beautiful girl, as the conviction rushed upon her mind that she had sacrificed herself for life!

Yet she faced the future that she had chosen for herself; faced it bravely, if desperately.

Mr. Mayhew had already secured tickets for New York, and checks for the four large trunks were obtained.   The train came in on time; and Ernest Mulford, bitterly reflecting later in the evening, was not

"I HAVE A VERY UNPLEASANT DUTY TO PERFORM, MR. MAYHEW."—Page 108.

comforted by the thought that, had he remained upon this train, he would have intercepted the pair at Bardwell, and saved all the exhaustion and peril of the night.

They took their seats in one of the cars, and the train sped on its way.

The cars were filled.   Mr. Mayhew, lost in the contemplation of his triumph and dimly forming plans for the future, lay back in the seat, and, possessing himself of June's hand, imagined himself happy.   He tried to engage her in conversation.   She answered in monosyllables and looked out of the window.

As the first hour of the journey neared its end, the whistle screamed for Randolph.   The train slowed up; the bell clanged; and the cars came to a stop at the station.

There was the bustle of passengers entering and leaving the train; there were the cries of hackmen and hotel-runners, and the rush of escaping steam from the engine.   June watched the flitting panorama outside, and listened to the cries, as some diversion from her own repressed misery.   Her face was still turned from her husband.   She became conscious that a tall man with a stick in his hand and a badge on his breast had stopped by their seat, and was conversing in low tones with Mr. Mayhew.

She could not hear their conversation.   If she had heard it, the following would have been its purport:

" Mr. Mayhew — you know me, don't you? "

" Ah — yes! — Mr. Jackman, the officer.   What do you wish? "

" Who is this with you? "

" My wife, sir."

" I thought so.   I've got a very unpleasant duty to perform, Mr. Mayhew.   I have a telegram to arrest you.   The train only stops five minutes; come at once, with the lady."

CHAPTER XXI.

AN ESCAPE.

" LET me see your telegram," said Mayhew. The officer handed it to him; he read it, as follows:

BARDWELL, Sept. 18, 9:50 P. M.
Station Police, Randolph:
Arrest Weston Mayhew; just left here on train; girl with him; charge, bigamy. Will come on next train, with warrant and officer.

EMMANUEL GREGORY.

The man had, at least, wonderful self-control. Now, when the dreaded thunderbolt at the last moment had descended upon him, he never quailed nor flinched. He neither paled nor flushed, nor did the hand shake that held the paper.

But he thought quickly, and his plan was instantly taken.

" It's a very unpleasant business for me, Mr. Mayhew," said the officer, in apology. " I hope there's some mistake about it. But you can explain it in the morning, when the warrant comes. Please hasten, sir; we haven't more than two minutes."

Weston Mayhew glanced at his wife. She was looking, without the least expression of interest, at the officer; she evidently had heard nothing of his talk.

" Excuse me a moment, June," said Mayhew; " I have a little business with this gentleman."

He rose and followed Mr. Jackman toward the car door.

" I don't want the lady disturbed," he explained. " Now, sir, I'll talk fast. You know me well, don't you, and have known me for years? "

"Yes, to be sure, Mr. Mayhew; and I trust you will——"

"Am I the kind of person that you are in the habit of detaining on an irresponsible telegram?"

"Why, no, Mr. Mayhew. We have to be very careful of taking such risks; but it was known here that you were to marry Mr. Gregory's daughter, and the telegram comes from him; so you see ——"

"It does *not* come from him!" He spoke with assured sternness and positiveness. "It is a base fabrication, the forgery of a worthless clerk whom I discharged a few weeks ago. He had the presumption to seek the hand of that lady, who is now my wife. He has done this out of revenge, to embarrass and annoy us both on our wedding journey. He would not dare to return to Bardwell if I were there, and I shall not find him there when I return. Mr. Gregory to send such a thing, indeed! Why, less than two hours ago I took his daughter yonder from his house, with the congratulations of himself and his wife."

The officer hesitated.

"Is it Ernest Mulford that you mean, sir?"

"Yes. That rascal robbed me, and now tries to annoy and humiliate me and mine."

"We heard something of his conduct, sir."

"You'll detain us at your peril, Mr. Jackman. You know that you are acting without authority, and assuming all the risk; and while ordinarily I would cheerfully comply with any reasonable request from an officer of the law, yet in such a case as this, where malice and hatred are trying to make you their tool to injure me, and at such a time, I declare to you that I will not go with you without a warrant. Short of that, you will have to use physical force; and I give you notice that if you do, I shall hold you responsible, both civilly and criminally, for assault and false imprisonment."

The voice of the conductor was heard: "All aboard!"

The officer looked as though he were not quite satisfied; but Mr. Mayhew's bold front and defiant words had produced their effect.

"I don't want to burn my fingers," he said. "I guess I'd better not meddle with this thing."

"You'll be wise if you don't," said the merchant, significantly. "Good evening, sir."

The engine-bell rang sharply. The train began to move. Mr. Jackman hastened to the platform and jumped off.

Mayhew drew a long breath. He took off his hat and wiped the perspiration from his brow with a silk handkerchief.

"A close call!" he thought. "I wonder who's at the bottom of it. Phebe, I suppose; I was afraid she'd show her claws at the last moment. Well, this settles one thing. I meant to stop over in New York to-morrow, day and night, but I shan't dare to now. An ocean steamer is my only safety now. Rather a rude honeymoon for the girl, but it can't be helped."

The train was under full headway again, when he resumed his seat by his bride. She turned her face to him. There was a change there; something in her looks that startled him.

"June, what's the matter?"

"Who was that man?"

Her voice was calm; but it was such a tone as Mayhew had never heard before.

"His name is Jackman."

"Is he a police officer?"

The powerful suppression of all emotion that he had shown before the officer failed him under her clear eye and direct questioning. He stammered and prevaricated.

"Why, yes — he was once, I think; but I —— "

"What was his business with you?"

"Come now, June, don't allow yourself to be disturbed by a trifle. I didn't mean to leave you so long; but this is the last call of business that I shall have before we get home again.   So, dearest wife, let us dismiss all care and give ourselves to happiness."

" Why did he not arrest you, as he wished to?"

He clutched the back of the seat with both hands, and stared at her.   Tightly grasped in her own hand, she held the tell-tale telegram up before his eyes.   He had dropped it on the floor when he walked away with the officer.

CHAPTER XXII.

IN SWIFT PURSUIT.

ERNEST MULFORD sprang up, and saw his uncle holding out a telegram, while his face was the picture of despair.   He snatched and read it.

RANDOLPH, SEPT. 18, 1877 — 10:15 P. M.
Emmanuel Gregory, Bardwell:

Can't take risk; no warrant.   Mayhew explains. They have gone with train.   Was dispatch yours?
ABEL JACKMAN.

" I waited at the station after sending my message," Mr. Gregory despondently explained, " and this is what we got; you see how it is.   That powerful scoundrel knows everybody, and he has bluffed off the police, some way.   Notice how this dispatch asks if mine was genuine!   I see how it is at once; he has made the police believe it a hoax."

" Well — didn't you telegraph the police at Beaverton?" Ernest impatiently asked.

" No; why should I?   It would only be a farce.   Such a man would defy arrest at Beaverton as easily as he has at Randolph."

" It is just as I said," put in Dr. Eldridge; " you've got to wait for his return.   It is sad, indeed, to think of poor June, and the heart-breaking news that will await her here on her completing her bridal tour; but there's no help for it.   It is the best we can do."

No person of Ernest Mulford's acquaintance, up to that time, had ever heard an oath from his lips.   Those who were about him heard one then, so vehement that they were startled.

"By God," it is not all we can do !   I will overtake that man this very night, and take June from him; I'll do it, or I'll die ! "

"Here's the coffee, Erny," said tearful Mrs. Gregory. " But you won't want it."

" I do want it, Aunty; it's just what I need.   I will take three minutes to drink it;" and he began to brace himself with the hot, fragrant Mocha.

" Doctor," he asked, " that's your horse and buggy that uncle has been using, isn't it? "

" Yes."

" Uncle, take it and go like lightning to Mr. Garland, the superintendent of this division of the road. He'll be at his house at this hour, I suppose.   Bring him here; tell him all about this villainy on the way, and then I will explain to him what I want.   Go, and return quickly.   I tell you there is hope yet."

" O, bless you, Erny!" said Mrs. Gregory.

Her husband put on his hat and was leaving the room, when a white, scared face was thrust in, and a woman's voice exclaimed in a painful shriek:

" O, Doctor! O, Doctor Eldridge! Come quick! She'll die before you can get there! "

" Well, what the devil is the matter now? " the doctor asked, with professional brusqueness.

The frightened woman, who looked and was dressed like a servant, was in a half-fainting condition, and hardly able to make herself understood.   The doctor went to her, and, by vigorous questions and a shake or two of her shoulders, succeeded in learning what was the trouble.

A Sharp Night's Work 8

" It is a serious matter," he said, in returning to
Ernest and his uncle. , " Indeed, it may be a matter of
life and death. I shall have to use my horse and
buggy myself."

" You can't have them," Ernest said, decidedly. " A
matter of life and death, do you say, Doctor? Here is
something more than a small question of mere life and
death. It concerns a woman's honor; it concerns the
apprehension of a great scoundrel; it concerns the happiness or misery of herself, of me, of both of you,
uncle and aunt, for our lifetimes. Do not talk to me
of a matter of life and death. Uncle, take the horse
and buggy, and bring Mr. Garland here quickly."

Long afterward the time came when the doctor could
calmly review the stirring, breathless incidents of that
night. He said that Ernest Mulford seemed to him, in
that hour, like a dictator giving his orders. He spoke
with the authority of absolute command.

" And I obeyed him, just as others did," he said,
" and gave up my horse and buggy, though I had
reason to think, from what I had just heard, that my
call was from a woman dying, if not actually dead."

So much dispatch did Mr. Gregory make that in less
than ten minutes Superintendent Garland was in the
parlor.

He was a man of business; he was all business —
accustomed daily to deal with the great and instant
problems of railroad traffic and travel, and to dispose
of them at a word.

" Mr. Gregory has told me all that has happened,"
he said, in a voice like the crack of a pistol. " I understand the situation perfectly. What do you want?"

" A special engine to catch the criminal," said Ernest.

" It will cost two hundred and fifty dollars," said the
superintendent.

" I'll pay it," Mr. Gregory shouted. But Ernest had
already taken out his wallet and counted out the amount.

The superintendent hastily recounted the bills and put them away.   Then he looked at his watch.

" You have a chance," he said.   " It is a slim one — and yet it is worth taking.   There is an up-grade from Randolph to Beaverton; that train is unusually heavy to-night; it won't make schedule time into twenty minutes or more.   It is now twenty minutes before eleven.   I can get you started in ten minutes, with an engineer who will do it if it can be done.   You'll have sixty minutes to make about eighty miles; for if you make Beaverton by twelve, you'll overhaul him.   But there is no time for affidavits, nor for getting warrants, nor deputy sheriffs.   You must start now, and alone. Will you? "

" Yes," said Ernest.   " Come! "

Mr. Gregory and his wife followed him to the door, both crying and bidding him God-speed.   He took his seat in the buggy with the superintendent, and they drove under the whip to the station.

Arrived there, the orders of the superintendent flew right and left, and the yards and buildings were astir with life.   A telegram went down the road to every station as far as Beaverton, giving warning of the coming of the special, and ordering the track to be cleared. An engine and tender steamed up to the station.

" All ready, Burt? " the superintendent sang out to the engineer, a thin, brown-faced young fellow, in shirt sleeves and overalls, who leaned from the cab window, with his hand on the lever.

" All ready, sir."

" Make the very best time to Beaverton that you can.   The *best time*, mark!   The track is clear; see what you can do with this engine that you brag so much about.   Good by, Mr. Mulford; if you don't overtake him at Beaverton, stop there and get the road cleared further.   I'll telegraph to help you.   Good luck to you! "

Ernest sprang into the cab and took the seat offered

him. The engine started. Within five minutes it was flying along at much less than a mile a minute. The spirit of Ernest Mulford rose. Hope swelled within him. The old refrain rose in his ears — " In time, in time! — kind God, in time! "

CHAPTER XXIII.

TOO LATE.

EVEN the fierce joy and exultation of Ernest Mulford's unconquerable spirit were hardly sufficient to hold him up against the apparent danger of this wild night-ride. Those dangers were more apparent than real; and yet, he who is borne upon a locomotive with only a tender following, over the rails at night, at a speed of much less than a minute to each mile—only such a one, we say, can understand his situation at this time.

He sat on the narrow seat by the window at the rear of the cab, his hand grasping the bell-cord. So fierce was the speed, so rapid the consumption of coal as it was continually shoveled into the glowing furnace, that the fireman was kept constantly busy, and Ernest had volunteered to take charge of the bell. His eye was fixed on Burt, the engineer, as he stood with one hand on the lever, peering out in front; stooping occasionally to examine the gauge, or turn a stop-cock. Now and then he sent out a deep whisper, " Ring! " With the voice of the bell answering to his pull, Ernest would hear the loud blast of the whistle, and in a twinkling the road-crossing would be passed. There was no stop, no slackening of speed; with a rush and a roar the engine swept on, making such a noise that at last the men in the cab had to shout to each other to be heard.

So tremendous became the speed, that the engine seemed to leap up from the track, and did really sway from side to side, so that Ernest had to hold on by the railing of the seat.

A multitude of lights flashed out far ahead. " Randolph! " the engineer shouted, as he let off the steam in a prolonged shriek. The engine dashed into town; it passed the station in a blaze of light, where, learning of the special on the way, a crowd of railroad employés and idlers lined the platform. As it tore past like a mad thing, the face of Burt at the lever was recognized, and he heard the shout that greeted him as the station was left far behind.

The miles sped past. The engineer was alert, vigilant, but silent. The fireman was busy at the coal. Ernest, keeping his eye on Burt, and unmindful of the oft-recurring bell-signal, had little time or thought for speech; but once, some distance out of Randolph, he leaned forward and yelled:

" Burt! — shall we make it? "

The engineer never turned his head; but above the awful clamor and noise the answer distinctly came:

" Yes! At this rate we shall reach Beaverton at eleven-fifty. I'll try and signal the train as we get near."

The whole ride to Ernest was like a nightmare; in the calm and peaceful nights that, later on, he knew, his sleep was often disturbed by flying phantoms with fiery eyes and flaming breath, born of the experience of this one night.

On, on they went. If ever on that memorable night Ernest ceased to think of the peril of June, it was while he was thus borne along so swiftly that even thought itself seemed left behind. Once the fireman, black and sooty from his labors, paused long enough to shout in his ear:

" You'll want to tell your children about this some day. No man before ever rode so fast on this road."

The lean, brown hand of the engineer reached back and pinched his knee.

"Look ahead!" he heard the cheery shout, rising above the noise. "There are the lights of Beaverton, three miles off; I'll signal."

A succession of sharp blasts from the whistle followed. Ernest was eagerly looking out ahead to see the rear lights of the train they were following, when a yell from the engineer startled him.

"Save yourselves! — she's going!"   .

The steam was released with a deafening roar; the motion was promptly reversed. The fireman, instantly comprehending the danger, leaped from the cab. His heels struck in the soft turf of the embankment over which engine and tender toppled together; two somersaults followed, and he landed on his back at the bottom of the bank, much shaken up, but not otherwise injured.

At the cry, and the toppling of the engine to the right, Ernest thrust himself through the window at his elbow. He went over with the huge mass, but above it, hanging on to the window aperture by his hands. He was jarred and shaken, but released his hold in time to escape the steam.

Struggling away from the wreck as it lay overturned, the ponderous wheels spinning in the air, Ernest was met by the fireman as he ran round the dismantled smoke-stack and came to the upper side.

"Where's Burt?" he screamed.

They searched for him. They saw his boots sticking out from the ruins of the cab. The axe was where it could be reached, protruding from the timbers and iron, and the fireman quickly chopped him free.

Poor Burt! He could not rise. He had inhaled the scalding steam, and was near to death. They dragged him out and laid him on the grass; he smiled to recognize them. With his mouth and throat all raw his poor remnant of breath and speech were freely given to the corporation that employed him.

"The flange of one of the drivers broke and flew

off," he whispered. " I saw it, and knew we must go. Tell my poor wife ——"

His brave spirit fled with the thought unuttered. He died as his class are ever ready to die, at the perilous post of duty.

It was no time for words nor explanations. Leaving the fireman kneeling by his dead friend, Ernest ran up the embankment, and along the track. The lights of Beaverton twinkled less than a mile before him. He ran with all the energy of despair. Putting into play all the poor reserve of wind, nerve and muscle that were left him, he hurried on. Nearer, nearer he came; he saw the lanterns at the rear of the train. He redoubled his efforts. He heard the ringing of the bell, the deep puff of the engine; he raised his voice in a shout that was not heard, and would not have been heeded had it been heard. One hundred yards from him the train pulled out, and with increasing speed left Beaverton behind.

" Merciful God, let me die!"

It was the frantic pursuer's despairing appeal, as he sank down.

CHAPTER XXIV.

BAFFLED!

WESTON MAYHEW looked in blank consternation at the telegram that June held up before his eyes. He clutched at it, but she was too quick for him. Holding her hands as far away from him as possible, she opened her hand-bag, thrust in the paper, and snapped the catch together. And then she faced him. It was a rigid, white face—like a beautiful stern image of mingled despair and resolution.

His face was stern, now, and he spoke through his teeth, in a hoarse whisper:

" Give me that paper."

" I shall not."

She grasped the bag tightly in both hands; she turned her back partly to him, to keep it from him.

" June, you are acting very wayward and silly. That dispatch belongs to me; I want it."

" It belongs to the policeman who ought to have arrested you. If you get it, you will have to take it from me by force. And if you do that I will scream, and appeal to the passengers."

He saw with dismay that she was roused, almost desperate; in such a frame of mind as he had not thought possible for this young, timid girl. He changed his tactics.

" I merely want to destroy it, June. It is carrying the joke too far to have that absurd thing in our possession."

" It is no joke."

" Why, you foolish girl, you don't believe a word of that lying message?"

" I believe every word of it. My father's name is on it."

" Your father never saw it, nor authorized it. The whole thing is a clumsy imposition; an attempt, I believe, of that scamp Mulford to annoy us both."

She was silent.

" I assure you that the statement of that message about me is a falsehood. You are my wife, the only wife I have ever had. Look at me, and say that you believe me!"

She did look at him. He read his doom in her steadfast eyes.

" Sir, I do *not* believe you! You are lying to me now, as you have been lying for months. This explains some things about your conduct that I could not understand. You would have this wretched day hastened; you would keep it quiet till almost the last moment. You are a villain, sir!—and I—I—O God!——"

She could not sustain the stress of desperate excitement that was upon her. She broke down, and sobbed in her handkerchief.

Weston Mayhew sat back in the seat, crushed his hat over his eyes, and collected himself for the struggle that was before him. Absorbing as had been his pursuit of this woman, it was not so overmastering as his determination to hold her, to carry her off, now that she seemed slipping from his grasp.

The low sound of her sobs reached the ears of some of the passengers, and inquiring eyes were turned that way. She threw a veil over her face.

Mayhew leaned over to her.

" Speak low," he said. " You do not want to attract attention, just now."

" I shall before long," she replied, her voice shaking with grief and agitation.

" Shall you, indeed! We'll see about that."

The devil within the man had begun to roar again.

" We'll have this thing understood at once, June. I have made my explanation to you of that annoyance back at Randolph. I am your husband; I am entitled to be believed. You say you don't believe me. Very well; I regret that; but it affects only your own peace of mind. It will do you no good; you will go right on with me to New York — and further. To-morrow you won't remember anything about it."

" To-morrow!" she moaned. " To-morrow! O, man, have pity on me! Let me go; I will go back to Bardwell alone. It is worse than death to stay with you; it is misery, shame and disgrace."

"As I just said," Mr. Mayhew coolly remarked, " we will go right on to New York. We reach there about the middle of the afternoon. I was expecting, my dear June, that we would remain a few days in the metropolis; I want to enjoy your charming society at one of its palatial hotels, as well as to show you some of the

sights; but I'm afraid we shall have to take passage
at once for Havre."

" For Havre?" she whispered.

" Yes, while this story abut me is a malicious fabrication, for which I will make somebody suffer when we
return to Bardwell, I don't choose to be annoyed by
it while on my bridal trip. I meant from the first to
make that trip a long one; and now, since this scoundrel, Ernest Mulford, or some other, has deliberately
set about trying to annoy and embarrass us in the midst
of our happiness, and might subject us to all kinds of
inconvenience in New York with these lying telegrams,
I have decided to put the ocean between us and these
absurd rumors. They will die a natural death long
before we return."

She tore the veil from her face, and confronted him
with eyes flashing with indignation.

" Sir, this is infamous! I am here with you now
only by the basest fraud and treachery; I will leave
this car and you at the next station."

" You will not."

" I will."

" Ah! You are my wife; the law makes you subject
to me. I hate to use force; if you compel me, I must.
You will keep this seat."

" I will alarm the passengers. I will appeal to the
conductor! Don't touch me, sir; I will scream."

Mr. Mayhew gave an irritating little chuckle.

" My dear little June, much as I admire your beauty,
I hate to see you in such a passion. Scream, will you?—
call on the conductor? — ask the passengers to take you
away from your husband? I don't wish you to do so,
because my explanation would be unpleasant, and the
incident an awkward one; but you are perfectly at
liberty to try it, for all the good it is likely to do you.
I am well acquainted with the conductor, and I know
several of the passengers in this car. How many of
them do you know? I should say, 'I fear that my

poor little wife is overcome and hysterical with excitement; I hope it may not affect her brain.' And I would sit by you with my arm about your waist — thus —" and despite her struggles he rudely embraced her, " and then we would see who would interfere."

There was silence after this rejoinder. Mr. Mayhew, sitting with his arm about June, thought that he had conquered her. He little knew the spirit that burns within the weak frame of a woman.

The train sped on; the whistle sounded for Beaverton, and the cars rolled into the station, fifteen minutes late.

Many passengers were to alight here; some were to get on. On the station platform there was quite a crowd, and much stir and bustle. The anxiety of those who were about to take the train to do so before those leaving it had got off, caused the usual confusion. The car platforms and aisles were full of people struggling to get on and off, and two or three lively newsboys selling papers increased the noise and movement.

One of these boys, crying his papers, passed by Mr. Mayhew.

" I'll take one," he said, having it in his mind that he would look for the departure of the ocean steamers.

To reach some loose change in his pocket, he found it convenient to rise. To examine it, it became necessary to step out into the aisle, where he could hold the silver up to the hanging lamp.

He felt some one brush against his back. This incident did not attract his attention at the instant, as people were still coming and going in the car.

He took his paper, received his change from the boy, and turned to take his seat.

The seat was vacant. June was gone!

He looked toward the nearest door. Very near it he saw the familiar blue feathers in her hat. At least ten people were between.

"Stop that woman!" he cried. "The woman with the round hat and blue feathers! Stop her!"

His cry startled the people, and, for the moment, added to the confusion. They looked round to see who was making the outcry, and their feet were stayed an instant. Continuing to cry, "Stop her—stop her!" Weston Mayhew crowded and forced his way with all the speed possible past the people who blocked the aisle, and reached the car platform. June had disappeared.

He jumped down and ran frantically through the crowd. He ran this way and that, getting himself cursed and almost collared for his rudeness. He looked for June in the crowd, in the waiting-rooms, in every hack and omnibus. She was not there.

He hurriedly described her dress to the policeman on duty.

"Didn't see no such person," was the brief reply.

He rushed along the train to where the baggage was fast being bumped out and in. The conductor stood by with his lantern.

"Give me ten minutes to find my wife, Mr. Sayles," the breathless searcher exclaimed. "I'm afraid she's out of her head. She got off the train and I can't find her."

"We shall be here about ten minutes more," said the conductor.

Quite ten minutes later Mr. Sayles walked from the ticket agent's office over to the train. The hacks and omnibuses and arriving passengers, who walked to their homes, had departed; the seats of the waiting train were almost filled; the crowd on the platform was thinned.

Mr. Mayhew came up again, strongly agitated and excited.

"I can't find her, conductor."

"Strange! Have you searched the train?"

"Yes; every car; baggage-cars, too. She's certainly not aboard."

"Well, I'm sorry; but you can't miss finding her here, somewhere."

"Can't you stop five minutes more?"

"Impossible; we are more than half an hour behind; we have time to make. Want your baggage?"

"No," said Mayhew. He had thought of that question, and settled it, as he excitedly pursued his search. "It'll be safe in New York; I shall come right on with her when I find her."

"All aboard!" the conductor shouted! The train pulled away and disappeared, Mr. Mayhew standing moodily by, and Ernest Mulford, a stone's throw back, sank exhausted, and cried out in his distress.

———

CHAPTER XXV.

LIGHT BREAKS.

IT was about two o'clock of the morning of September 19th. At the Ashley House, the first hotel in Beaverton, and a comfortable inn of the country kind, something unusual seemed to have happened. The office was lighted and the proprietor was sitting up. He had sent his help to bed and was sleepily trying to fulfill an unusual demand upon his house, which he foresaw would become a matter of profit.

Mr. Emmett Ashley was a young man of about twenty-seven, rotund, round-faced, cheerful in talk and demeanor, and with good business capacity; in brief, was excellently equipped to be just what he was — the successful landlord of a good country inn. There was that about the house itself, its ways, its table, and especially its host, that brought traveling people to it, and gave it a name. On rare occasions, such as this, Mr. Ashley could deprive himself of sleep in the interest of his business, but he did not like to do so, and the occasion must be a large one to persuade him to forego even a part of that daily luxury.

The house was silent; the town was still. Mr. Ashley yawned, stretched, walked about the room, whistled, slapped his hands, and resorted to some other expedients known to sleepy people who wish to stay awake. He found it rather hard work.

"Plague take such unreasonable people who put off having trouble till the middle of the night, and keep decent people awake to attend to 'em. I'm going to lie down any way; they'll find me here when they come."

He threw himself down on a settee, and was speedily unconscious of the troubles of hotel-keeping. The sound of the opening and closing of the office door awakened him. He opened his eyes and saw a man advancing to the counter.

"When does the next train leave here for New York?" the visitor asked.

"Nine-thirty."

The man looked at the clock.

"More than seven hours yet," he sighed, and sank wearily into a chair.

Mr. Ashley thought he recognized the voice. He stood up and looked at the man in the chair. His attitude and appearance were those of deep dejection. His chin was on his breast, his eyes fixed on the floor, and his hat was drawn down on his face.

Mr. Ashby gave a soft little exclamation of astonishment, and walking round the counter, bestowed a resounding whack upon the shoulders of the other. The sitter started to his feet.

"Well, Ernest—how are you?" the landlord asked, and held out his hand.

"Why, it's Emmett!" exclaimed the other, unexpectedly finding himself interested in what was going on about him. "Do you keep this house?"

" Yes, my son, I do that, and have for more than a year. Hadn't you heard of it?"

" I knew there was somebody of the name here, but never thought it could be my old schoolmate."

They shook hands and sat down. Then Mulford's great grief came back to him, and he became silent and moody.

" See here, now," said the landlord, in his cheery way, being now wide awake, " what are you in the dumps about? Did you get in at half-past eleven — and if so, where have you been since, and what do you want, any way? It gives me the blues to look at you."

" I'm tired enough to go to bed," replied Ernest, " and I would, if there was any prospect that I could sleep; but I know I can't. I've been roaming around the streets for most two hours, and came in here because I saw a light. I'll sit here, with your leave, 'till morning."

" What are you driving at?"

" I've been chasing up the biggest scoundrel in the State all day, and just missed him here with a special engine. I'm bound to keep after him, and I shall go on in the morning; but I've little hope now. He'll have more than nine hours start."

" Why — did you come in on that engine that ran over the bank and killed the engineer, just below here?"

" Yes — and barely missed the train here. I wish now I had been in the engineer's place."

" Don't be a fool, Ernest! One of the railroad men came in here, half an hour ago, and told me of that accident; but I don't think the news has got around here yet."

Ernest Mulford said nothing.

" Who's your man? "

" Weston Mayhew."

" WHAT! "

The emphasis that Mr. Ashley put upon the word made Mulford start in his chair.

" Say that again! "

· The name was repeated.

" What's *he* been doing? "

Ernest looked wearily at his inquisitive friend.

" You can't help me, Emmett, in my distress; so it will be of no use to tell you."

" How do you know I can't be of use to you?   Just you start in and tell me all about it, and, just as like as not, something will come of it.' "

Without the   slightest expectation that anything could " come of it " — but to pass away the time, to relieve his own sorely-burdened heart by speech, and very possibly out of a yearning for the sympathy that he knew hearty Emmett Ashley would give him, Ernest Mulford told him everything, beginning with his own leaving of Bardwell, of which Ashley had not heard. The latter listened intently to the strange and exciting story, and at its close uttered a peculiar whistle.

" The damned scoundrel ! " he exclaimed.   " Have you got those documents with you, Ernest? "

" Yes."

" Do you mind showing them to me? "

The package was handed to him.   He looked it over and returned it.

" I suppose," he remarked, " that you are pretty familiar with that man's writing? "

" Yes, of course."

" Just step this way."

He led him to the counter and pointed to the open register.   Under the new date, " September 19th,'' he saw in well-known characters the name, " Weston Mayhew."

" Emmett! — is he here? "

" Yes."

" And she —— "

He stopped; he could ask no more.

" No. But see here, Ernest — get that wolfish look off your face. I won't have any shooting or stabbing in this house. Promise me there shall be no violence, or I'll not help you an atom.

" I'll do anything you say, Emmett; but tell me where June is."

" I'll tell you all I know. About a quarter past twelve Weston Mayhew, whom I knew by sight, came in after the other arrivals on the train had come and gone to bed. He was a good deal excited; said that his wife had been taken ill and delirious on the train, and had given him the slip after it stopped here. He had searched the train through and all about the station, and could find nothing and hear nothing of her. He gave me fifty dollars; wanted me to get together a dozen men to help find her, and to keep open till she was found, so that she might have all necessary attention. He said he should go on with her — *must* was the word he used — by the morning train, and he wanted my help; perhaps he should want a doctor. Before he had got through talking he threw down another fifty. I agreed, of course; everything appeared straight. He started out with a lot of men that I got for him, to hunt the town through. Didn't you come across any of them?"

" As I roamed through the streets I continually met men who seemed to be searching; but I heard nothing of what it meant, and I did not see Mayhew. Perhaps it's just as well that I did not."

" Why?"

" I might have killed him."

" Tut, tut, sonny ——"

" He ought to be shot on sight," Ernest passionately interrupted, "and I'm none too good to do it! Just think of all I have told you; it makes my blood boil. I thank God that she has escaped him; the news you have told me makes me a happy man, compared with

A Sharp Night's Work 9

what I was when I came in here; but think of June; I don't believe that the monster lied when he told you that she was sick and out of her head; the poor girl has learned enough of him since he took her from her father's house, only six hours ago, to make any woman crazy. Think of the dear girl wandering in the darkness of the night, fleeing from that villain, and trying in vain to find shelter and protection among strangers! I'll go at once to find her. I will protect her and take her back to her home."

He started up, and made for the door. The landlord held him by the collar.

"Attend to me, Ernest," he said. "All that can possibly be done to find her is being done. You can do nothing, except to bring on a collision between Mayhew and yourself, which must not occur just yet. If she is found, she will be brought here; it will be time for you to appear. If she is not found, I shall know what intelligence of her has been gained. Of course, now that I have heard your story and seen your proofs, I am hand and glove with you in bringing the man to justice, and setting June right. Only, I don't want you to appear yet. The time has not come. Go in there and lie down on the bed. I will let you know when he returns, and what the news is; and then we will consult about what to do. But you *must* stay in the background for the present."

Much against his will, Ernest was forced into a little room adjoining the office behind the counter, and the door was closed after him. He threw himself on the bed, and was almost instantly asleep. Nature would assert her rights.

He was awakened by the hand of his friend, who had to shake him roughly before his deep slumber was broken. Ashley was standing by the bed, with the door closed.

"Is she found?" Ernest eagerly asked.

"She will be, very soon. It is now six o'clock; a

market-gardener who just came in met a woman some miles out in the country that answers her description. They are hitching up now to go after her. Don't get up yet; let me talk, and tell you my plan. I've hit on the proper thing to do."

" But I won't stay here. I tell you ———. "

" Keep still, boy, and hear my plan."

The stout friend told his plan.

———

CHAPTER XXVI.

IN DARKNESS AND DISTRESS.

JUNE'S complete disappearance is naturally and easily explained. Had not Mr. Mayhew been so agitated and excited in the first moments of his search, that explanation must have occurred to him.

Reaching the car-platform in the press of people struggling to come and go, the fugitive glanced from the blaze of light on the station-side to the street opposite, on the other side of the train, and observed with that glance that it was but dimly lighted with a gas-lamp here and there, and that hardly anybody was moving upon it. Nobody was getting on or off on that side, and a sudden impulse came to her that safety lay that way. She acted upon it instantly. She had reached the ground and disappeared before Mayhew was able to get to the car-door.

The determination not to go with her oppressor and tyrant beyond this station had been formed an hour before. Her resolution to escape from the fate that he had coolly portrayed to her was something ardent, irresistible; she would have obeyed it had it urged her through fire and water. She was about to " make a scene " when the train stopped; to shriek and cry out for help; to denounce Mayhew as a criminal, and to those who would gather around upon the disturbance, to show the telegram in confirmation of her words.

That plan might and might not have succeeded; it is impossible to say. She had to deal with an experienced man of the world, of smooth and easy address, and full of resources. People generally, traveling people especially, always intent upon their own affairs, and anxious to prosecute their journey without interruption or annoyance, are loth to interfere in others' troubles. Then Mr. Mayhew was well acquainted with the conductor, and probably could have made him believe that the lady was out of her head. The chances are that the desperate plan that June suddenly formed as she saw her companion rise and go into the aisle was the best that she could, under the circumstances, have adopted. And whether the comings and goings of that memorable night were ruled by mere chance, or by a higher power, it is certain that this course was the only one that could put it in the power of her heroic pursuer on the crippled engine to reach her. All unknown to her, she was doing just what he would have had her do.

She passed rapidly up the street to the first corner, meeting no one. She turned the corner, ran along that street, turned another corner to a street where there was no light but the faint and uncertain rays from the windows, and pressed on till breath and strength failed her. Then she sank down on a doorstep and rested.

One swift thought of her condition came to her. Barely four hours before the petted darling of a happy home, the honored bride of a great and wealthy man; now outcast, wretched, filled with terror, flying from the pursuit of a monster, a criminal, whose very touch would degrade her! Just one thought like this she allowed herself, and then she crushed it down and tried to take courage from the other thought: " I am escaping him. I will find refuge and shelter somewhere, and send news to my father, and he will come and take me home."

She had a thought, too, for another, in that distressful, yet excited hour. She thought how different all this might have been had she listened to Ernest Mulford's suit. But that thought belonged to the bygones; she sighed and dismissed it.

Far down the street she heard the unsteady steps of some late roysterer on his homeward way. Full of the terror inspired by the thought of Mayhew's pursuit, she sprang up and continued her flight. On, on she sped, past the straggling outskirts of the town, and into the country; along the highway, past farmhouses and cornfields, and once through a thick, dark wood, where the gloom increased her terrors, redoubling her pace as her imagination constantly conjured up the sound of feet or wheels in pursuit. Faint, footsore, utterly exhausted, she fell helplessly on the steps of a large house close to the road. It was a country inn, the landlord of which was waiting on a merry party in the bar. He heard the noise caused by the poor wanderer stumbling against the steps, and he opened the door. In the light that shone upon her woful face, she looked up to him for pity — and found none.

"Out of this, now, you baggage!" the brutal man harshly exclaimed, with his foot raised. "We want no tramps or slatterns around here. Off with you!"

She rose with difficulty. Some of the revelers inside crowded up and looked over the landlord's shoulders. One, a fashionably-dressed youth, with flushed face and disordered dress, elbowed his way past.

"Why, she's pretty!" he hiccoughed; "or she was once, any way. Landlord, g'way, and le' me have her. Come right in, my little dear. Come with me ——"

With a cry of horror, and with strength supplied by the insult, she fled on into the darkness, followed by jeering shouts from the doorway.

Thus she struggled on her painful flight, and the tedious hours wore on toward the dawn. Her strength was all spent, her tender feet were bruised and blistered by the hard road, her dress was torn, and her hair, escaping from its confinement, fell unkempt over her shoulders. More than once she cast herself down by the wayside, resolved to go no further; anon, the thought of Weston Mayhew, and perhaps some noise down the road, would nerve her again, and she would toil on a little further.   Before the tardy daylight came, several early market carts on the way to Beaverton had met and passed her, and she noticed others when it was light enough to see them.   And she dragged herself on.

The sun was just rising when she stopped and leaned upon the low palings of a pretty little cottage.   A women was milking a cow inside the fence, while a little girl played near her.

" O mamma," she cried, " See the poor lady! "

The woman looked over her shoulder.

" Come here instantly, May," she called, " and let the miserable creature be."

She went on with her milking.   June knew that a rude rebuff waited for her; but blows could not have driven her away then.   She had not strength to move.

The woman finished her milking, and rose from the stool.   She frowned upon seeing June still at the fence.

" What do you want?" she asked, in a hard voice.

" I am sick and tired," was the answer.   The speaker looked wistfully at the pail.

The woman took a tin cup from the pump, and dipping it full of the unstrained milk, handed it to June.   She drank it eagerly, and in a faint voice said, " More."

" Why, you poor creature! " the other cried, as she again filled the cup.   " You're almost famished.   Are you hungry? "

June again emptied the cup, and returned it, with a look of the deepest gratitude.

" A little," she answered, " but more weary.   I can hardly stand; I — I believe I am going to faint."

She would have fallen where she stood, had not the compassionate woman sprung outside and supported her in her arms. She directed the little girl to bring her some water from the pump in the cup, and she revived June by throwing a little of it into her face.

The sorrowful blue eyes opened gratefully upon her. "Thank you," whispered June. "You are very kind."

"You poor creature, I can't help pitying you, even if you are bad," the woman said.

June thrust her indignantly away.

"I have done nothing wrong," she said. "I am pursued and persecuted by a wicked man, and I will kill myself sooner than go with him."

"Dear me!" cried the woman. "Forgive me; I believe you. You look like a lady. How far have you walked?"

"From Beaverton."

"Beaverton! Lord save you! — it's almost ten miles. Come right in."

She almost carried her into the house.

CHAPTER XXVII.

REFUGE AND DISCOVERY.

JUNE seemed in a moment to be transported from the depths of misery and suffering of mind and body to the height of security and comfort. The heart of the good housewife was touched for her, and she seemed unable to do enough to show her sympathy.

"Don't say a word," she said, as she bustled about. "I feel grieved and provoked at myself that I didn't see at once that you was good, and only in trouble on account of some dreadful man. Oh, these men! I tell my Wally that there ain't more than one out of ten of 'em that can be trusted; but Wally is a jewel; yes, indeed, he is. Don't you talk now, I say, for you're weak and sick, and mustn't exert yourself till I fix you

up, and get a little strength into you. After awhile
you shall tell me all about it, and we will see what's to
be done; but I'm going to have my way with you for a
while."

The kind soul laid June upon her own bed, brought
her a basin, soap and towels, insisted on bathing her
swollen and lacerated feet with her own hands, and
combed out her long brown hair, admiring its thickness
and its rich hue. In a few minutes she had prepared
tea and toast for her.

"Now, lie right down there, and go to sleep," was
the next gentle command, after June had partaken of
the refreshment. She gladly yielded, and soon forgot
her troubles in a deep, tranquil slumber.

It lasted more than two hours. The clock was
striking twelve when she awoke and came out into the
neat little sitting-room.

"You're looking ever so much better," said the
woman. "Here's an easy pair of slippers for your
poor feet. Sit down in that easy-chair, and if you feel
well enough, you may tell me about yourself. I'm
Mrs. Bartram; my husband owns fifty acres of land
here; you can almost see from the back-door where
he's at work in the fields, with three men. I must get
dinner for 'em; but I've plenty of time. They got an
extra good start this morning; I was up before daylight, getting their breakfast. Are you strong enough
to talk?"

In a few words June told her story. The simple
country life of Mrs. Bartram had made her acquainted
with no such experience as this, and she was deeply
moved by it. At times her cheeks flamed with indignation, and then tears of sympathy rolled down
them.

"You poor, dear, abused child!" she cried, when
June had done. "And you're only nineteen! — and
were just married last night! — and that brute — that
monster ——"

She stopped, because she could not find words with which to express her wrath, and she clinched her fingers, and went through with a pantomime that looked much like the pulling of hair.

"But don't worry, my dear lady; you are safe now," she added.

"You don't know that dreadful man," said June, with a shudder. "He'll never give up till he finds me, and then he'll take me away by force."

"By force, will he?" spunky little Mrs. Bartram echoed. "I'd like to see him — in *this* house! I'd take the broomstick to him, if there was no man about; and just wait till noon, and Wally'll be home with the men, and one of them shall stay with us all the rest of the day."

"I would like to send a telegram to my father," said June.

"So you shall. Wally shall send one of the men over to Beaverton with it after dinner; he'll get it right off, of course?"

"Yes," interrupted June, hopefully, "and then he can start from Bardwell a little after nine to-night, and get to Beaverton before twelve. Oh, do send it for me!"

"Patience, little one," said Mrs. Bartram. "Everything is going on all right. The man will take it over after dinner. If I should go out into the fields now for him, I'd have to leave you alone, and that you wouldn't like."

"No — no!"

"Of course not. Get the telegram written. There's paper and pen and ink. Tell your father that you're safe, and that he can find you at Wallace Bartram's, nine miles out on the Hillsdale road."

June wrote the message, while her kind hostess busied herself about the room. When she had finished it she laid it on the table, saying:

There's a little money in my bag; you may——"

"Don't talk about money, please," interrupted Mrs. Bartram. "Wally will see that it goes. Now, if you are comfortable, just sit here and amuse yourself, while I do my kitchen work and get the dinner going for those men. My, how hungry they do get! Here's books and papers; if you want anything, rap on the table; I shall be sure to hear you. Wally says I've got the quickest ear and the sharpest tongue of any woman in the country."

She ran into the kitchen, laughing.

June turned the leaves of some of the books, and looked at the pictures, but she could not get interested in them. The cheerful words of Mr. Bartram had strengthened her and calmed her fears, and her thoughts were turning to the coming of her father, her meeting with him, and her journey back to her old home. Knowing nothing of the facts of Mayhew's crimes, with no information except what was given by the dispatch in her bag, yet a feeling had crept into her breast that Ernest Mulford was in some way connected with the discovery, and that she should see him when she returned to Bardwell

She was so deeply immersed in her thoughts that she did not hear or see a double-carriage drive up to the cottage from which three men alighted. One of them came rapidly up to the open door. His shadow on the floor startled her; she looked up and saw Weston Mayhew.

CHAPTER XXVIII.

RETRIBUTION AND REUNION.

"COME!" he said.

She strove to rise, but her limbs failed her. She put her hands before her face to shut out his hateful presence.

"Come, you foolish creature!" he continued, with

hardly the appearance of tenderness. "Come along with me. You have made me much trouble, and I have had a long search for you; but it turned out just as it was certain to. Let me tell you now, once for all, such conduct will do you no kind of good. You may succeed in severely trying my patience, as you have now, putting us back on our journey almost a day; you may possibly, if you continue such conduct, lessen my devotion to you; but you will still remain my wife, subject in all things to my control. Come, I say!"

She knew it would be useless to argue with him; she did not try it. But there was one appeal she could make.

"I am sick and weak, and my feet are blistered with my long walk. I cannot go."

He gave a sardonic grin.

"Very cool of you, June, I think, to remind me of your bad condition, which you brought upon yourself by trying to run away from me. But that will not avail. I have brought some stout fellows along to help me, in case you should resist; they will be useful now to carry you to the carriage. Wait; on second thought, I'll carry you out myself. I don't choose to have this very shapely form in the arms of any man but myself. I shall take you to the hotel at Beaverton; we will remain there till the next train, and then we will go on. I will engage a berth in the sleeping-car for your comfort. Come!"

He had been standing by the door; he stepped forward now, with outstretched arms, to take her up. She screamed, and rapped the table sharply with her knuckles.

Mrs. Bartram appeared. At one glance she comprehended the situation. She boldly placed herself between June and Mayhew.

"What do you want here?" she demanded.

"I want my wife. Get out of the way."

"She is not your wife.   I know all about you.
You can't take her out of this house.   I defy you to
lay a finger on her."

Angered by this unexpected opposition, Mayhew
took Mrs. Bartram by the shoulders, and thrust her
rudely to one side.   Her blood was up, and rushing to
the kitchen, she reappeared in an instant with the tongs.
She would certainly have attacked the man before her
with them, but she caught sight through the door of
two more men coming up from the carriage.   Catching
up her child in her arms, she ran though the kitchen
out into the fields, screaming, " Wally! Wally! " at the
top of her voice.

June clutched the arms of the chair with her feeble
hands.

" I will not go willingly," she said.   " You will have
to tear me away."

" It will be unpleasant to use force; but if I must —"

" You will use no force toward this lady."

One of the men had entered the house, and placed
himself between the man and his intended victim.   He
spoke quietly, but with decision, and in a voice that
seemed strangely familiar.

The heart of June Gregory leaped at the sound, but
there was nothing familiar in the man's appearance.
As he stepped forward to interfere, she saw that he had
a bristling shock of fiery red hair, and a green shade
over his eyes.

" Get back, you meddlesome cur! " Mayhew savagely
commanded, with a peremptory wave of his hand.
" Who called on you?   Who told you to come into the
house?   I'll let you know when you are wanted."

The red wig and the green shade came off, and were
thrown at Mayhew's feet.   The man stood with folded
arms, looking calmly at his baffled enemy.

Ernest Mulford was revealed!

With bloodshot eyes and face, with open mouth;

panting like a beast, and with clenched fists, Weston Mayhew was about to rush upon him.

"Beware!" Mulford exclaimed. "If you come this way, you'll get hurt. I don't want to strike you. I can't control myself, and if I strike you, I may kill you."

"I guess I will take a hand here," the other man said in a loud voice, coming forward and placing a hand on the enraged Mayhew's shoulder. "Weston Mayhew, I arrest you. Don't resist; if you do, I shall put these trinkets on you."

Realizing that the game was played out, that he had lost in the desperate hazard that he had staked everything upon, the baffled villain even in that threatening moment showed a bold front and an insolent air.

"Leave the house, sir, till I call you! Damnation! what do you fellows whom I have hired to help me mean by intruding yourselves in this way?"

"Drop that," said the man who held his hand firmly on the other's shoulder. "That cock won't fight. You are the victim of one of Ern Ashley's clever tricks. He has helped me take you; but I should have had you before the day was out, any way."

"Who are you?"

"My name is Matt Garton. I am under-sheriff of the county. That young man over there is my deputy, specially authorized for this occasion."

"What do you claim the right to arrest me for?"

"Bigamy. I could hand you over to the United States marshal for all kinds of deviltry with the mails, but I don't think he'll have a chance at you for quite a while yet."

"I'll trouble you to produce your warrant."

"I'll trouble you to come out and get into that carriage, and go back to Beaverton with me, and you'll be shown my warrant without any delay. In short, Mr. Mayhew, I'll submit to no nonsense with you. I know what the evidence is on which the warrant is to be got; I've seen a great part of it myself, in writing, and I'm not going to take any chances of your getting away."

"But I won't submit without process.   I'll fight for my liberty first."

The officer instantly drew a revolver, cocked it and covered Mr. Mayhew's head.

"Mr. Mulford," he said, in a cold, stern voice, "take these handcuffs and put them on that man.   I'll stand no talk from him of resistance and fighting the officers of the law."

With his heart almost bursting with rage, Mayhew submitted to the unspeakable humiliation of having his triumphant and deeply-injured rival handcuff him like a felon.

"You'll all smart for this," he threatened, with such thick utterance that his speech resembled the growl of a wild beast.   "You have no evidence."

"You might as well know," said Mulford, "that I have in my pocket at this moment the certificate of your marriage with Phebe Bashford, more than ten years ago, and that that marriage will be amply proved.   I have also in my pocket, restored and legible, all the letters that I wrote from Granby to Bardwell, to this lady and others, and one letter which she wrote to me and which you abstracted from the post-office, opened, read, and destroyed.   They were all found in your waste-basket, and pieced together; and at least one of them you were seen to read and destroy.   What are you going to say to that?"

Like the knell of doom did this revelation sound in the ears of the guilty man.   Knowing the blind infatu-ation of Phebe for him, he had been reasoning since his interview with the police-officer at Randolph, that she had probably dropped some hint of the truth, in her vexation at his marriage with June, and that it had come to the ears of Ernest Mulford; but he *knew* that this woman would never make such a charge openly

against him, nor confirm it if made by others, and he
had been easy in his mind as to that accusation, except
for the temporary inconvenience that it gave him.

But now he was confronted with the written proof of
that marriage, which, with too great caution, he had
neglected to destroy when he had discovered it; and
with those fatal letters, which he had supposed were
burned up by Blynn!

He stared at Mulford.   One faint ray of hope darted
to his brain.   Was not this merely assertion, born of
suspicion, made to induce a confession?   Was it not a
trap that was skillfully set for him?

" It is all false!" he said, defiantly.   " There never
were any such things in existence.   I defy you to produce them!"

Ernest Mulford took out the strong envelope.

One by one the damning proofs of his guilt were
held up within a yard of his face, while he stood with
helpless hands and raging brain, overwhelmed by the
torrent of his crushing defeat.

His startling situation and its consequences flashed
upon him with horrible distinctness.

He was defeated, discovered, at all points.

The things that men call honor, respect, admiration,
the names of which he had enjoyed to his fill, were
utterly gone.

June was lost to him; June, the peerless, priceless
creature, for whom he had risked all.   Aye, unhappy
man — you never had really and truly possessed her!

He could not even enjoy the stealthy love of Phebe
Bashford, his real wife.   There would have been a cer-
tain charm in that, if he could still have possessed it.
But he could not.

It must go with the rest; his wealth could not save
him; he must lose that, too, for years and years —
perhaps for the balance of his lifetime.

Because the prison-gates were yawning for him.

There could be no escape.   Repeated crimes had in-
sured his doom.

The strain was too much.   A blood-vessel burst in
his brain.   The terrible grasp of apoplexy was laid
upon him, and smote him helpless to the floor.

CHAPTER XXIX.

SUNSHINE THROUGH CLOUDS.

MR. GARTON knelt down by the prostrate man,
loosened his vest and collar, and called for water to
dash in his face.   He did not move.   The officer's
hand explored the breast for the heart.   There was not
the faintest beat.

" He is dead," was the brief comment.

June bowed her face upon her hands, and saw that
odious face no more.

Brisk Mrs. Bartram stormed into the house from the
rear, with her stalwart husband, in his shirt-sleeves,
and three laborers following.   In a few words, whispered aside, Ernest Mulford explained the situation.

The body was carried into another room.

" Things have taken an unexpected turn," said Mr.
Garton.   " My authority is at an end — and yours, too,
Mr. Mulford.   I will go back to Beaverton, and notify
the coroner and the undertaker."

" And please telegraph the news, briefly, to Emmanuel Gregory, Bardwell, and ask him to come on
here."

" I will, sir.   Good-day."

Death, under any roof, produces a hush.   It did
here.   One of the men was sent in to remain with
the corpse, and Wally Bartram and the others stood
around in the kitchen, and heard the housewife's nar-
rative of what she had seen and what June had told
her, while the preparations for dinner went on; for men
must dine, though death be in their midst.

June, in the sitting-room, looked up, and saw Ernest standing near.

"You heard what I said to that man," he said. "You will know, then, what villainy has kept us apart, and slandered my good name; yes, and almost made us both wretched for life. When you know how I have labored and struggled to shield you from that man and save you from a fate that would shadow your life forever, you will understand better than I could tell you two months ago, better than I can now tell you, how much I love you. But perhaps you have not changed your mind. If not, I can leave you with my blessing, though with a heavy heart."

He turned partly away. He heard her pronounce his name.

"Ernest!"

She was holding forth both hands to him. Tears of gratitude and affection were falling from her eyes, through which a little smile broke like the sun through the clouds.

Mrs. Bartram, thinking that June might be wanting something by this time, looked into the sitting-room. She softly reclosed the door, and came back into the kitchen.

"It is all right," she said to the men. "I had a lively suspicion that the clever fellow who took off the wig, as we've heard, was the dear girl's own young man; and now I *know* it. Such hugging and kissing I haven't seen since — since —"

"I know what you mean," said Wally; and she boxed his ears with a wet hand.

After midnight Mr. Gregory reached the cottage. We draw a veil over the meeting between him and his child and Mulford.

It was three days before June had sufficiently recovered from the fatigues and exposures of that dreadful night to be able to travel. The little cottage was put to its

A Sharp Night's Work 10

utmost capacity during that time to hold the guests; but Mrs. Bartram proved herself equal to the emergency.

The coroner's jury examined into the cause of Weston Mayhew's death, and found that it was due to natural causes. The body was sent to Bardwell, and there buried.

Upon his person, at the time of his death, there was found the sum of ten thousand dollars in paper money, and drafts on New York for forty thousand more. At the instance of a creditor to whom he owed several hundred dollars, a temporary administrator of his estate was appointed. The trunks of the deceased were returned from New York to this person, and an examination of their contents showed a little more than one hundred and fifty thousand dollars, in registered United States bonds, foreign exchange and certificates of stock.

Thus again was the sagacity of the detective in his predictions to Ernest Mulford confirmed.

As the train that brought home Mr. Gregory and his daughter and Ernest rolled into the station, it seemed as though half the population of Bardwell, men, women and children, were there. And when these three stepped from the car they were at once surrounded by a crowd of eager, sympathizing faces. Mr. Gregory soon got June into a carriage, and took her home to its rest and seclusion, and to the embrace of her mother. Ernest could not escape so easily. For once a whole community seemed struck with something like shame at having credited the vile slanders against a worthy man, and turned out to welcome him back in honor. The astounding facts connected with the death of Bardwell's foremost citizen, the intelligence of his crimes, and the heroic struggle of Ernest, so strangely crowned with success at last, to save June from him, had created something like a popular furor for the young man. The people now besieged him with their congratulations and praises. The men shook him by the hand until his arm ached, called him a splendid fellow, and hoped for him all kinds of good fortune. The ladies would have their say, too; his had been that kind of self-sacrificing devotion that always appeals strongly to the female heart; and in that hour he was so lionized that he wearied of it.

The whole truth must be told. Many of the ladies were so enthusiastic that they insisted on kissing him, and had their will.

When the excitement had partially subsided, a friendly voice said:

"Let me add my congratulations, now, Mr. Mulford; you have done splendidly."

"Ah — Mr. Lear!" exclaimed Ernest, heartily shaking his hand. "When did you get here?"

"On the next day, the 19th, as I expected. The attack passed off, as I anticipated. I learned by telegraph at Granby Station what had happened, and the ardent pursuit you were making. It was precisely the thing; nobody could have advised anything better.

"I saw that everything was going to turn out as it should. About seven, when Mayhew was unsuspiciously starting out with you and the sheriff in his carriage, Mr. Ashley sent a dispatch, and at noon we got another from the sheriff, telling the whole story."

The two men had escaped from the crowd and were walking arm in arm toward the hotel.

"And all that I have done," said Ernest, with deep emotion, " would have been of not the least avail had not your skill and perseverance unraveled all that man's villainy so promptly and secretly, and put me on the track in time to run him down, and save June. Excellent man! —how can I ever begin to repay you? And why have you taken such an interest in my welfare — and hers?"

They passed beneath a lamp and Ernest saw one of

his serious smiles softening the hard lines around the detective's mouth.

"No matter about that now, Mr. Mulford. There's time enough yet for that explanation. At present I would like to ask a question of you, if you will not think it impertinent."

"After what has happened, you could not possibly be impertinent about my affairs."

"You encourage me to ask the question, and it is a delicate one. I do not ask it out of idle curiosity, mind! The answer very deeply concerns your welfare in more than one point of view. I would like to know if the misunderstanding has been removed between Miss Gregory and you."

"Entirely," replied Ernest.

The detective was silent.

"Perhaps you'd like to know something more?" the young man laughed.

"Indeed, I would very much like to know one thing more."

"Then you shall. June and I are engaged. While there could not with propriety, at this stage of our affairs, be a definite engagement and a day fixed, yet everything is clear between us, and if we both live a few months longer, we shall be man and wife."

Mr. Lear seized both his hands and wrung them.

"My dear fellow, I am rejoiced to hear it. I congratulate you again, because," and the serious smile broadened over his face, "you are about to hear a most astonishing piece of news, for which you could not possibly have been prepared."

CHAPTER XXX.

A HORROR OF THE NIGHT.

WHEN, on the night of the 16th of September, Weston Mayhew went to the house of Mrs. Bashford and vainly tried to gain admittance, for the purpose of stealthily possessing himself of the marriage certificate, the house was in fact vacant. Its mistress had gone to Randolph that morning, and did not return till the morning following. Emilia, her domestic, had been allowed to go home in the meantime, and came back on the 17th. So frequent were these occasions that the girl was requested to absent herself for a brief time, growing mainly out of the secret visits of Mayhew to the house, that she had come to think nothing of them. The real truth she never dreamed of. She rather liked her mistress, though regarding her as an eccentric kind of person, and since she received excellent wages, and the work was light, so much liberty was quite agreeable to her.

The 17th passed as usual with Mrs. Bashford and her domestic. Things went on as usual in that house on the next day, till after the dinner hour. About three o'clock the little bell summoned the servant to the parlor.

Mrs. Bashford was sitting in the depths of a great easy chair, with a large volume on her lap.

"I shall not want you till to-morrow, Emilia," she said. "Go home now."

"You'll wish me to be here to get the breakfast, ma'am, won't you?"

"To get the breakfast?" repeated the lady.

The girl said afterward that her mistress spoke as if she did not comprehend the very simple question, and seemed to look away beyond her, in a vacant kind of way. Her eyes returned to the book; she did not answer the question at all. Emilia left her, more than ever convinced that, kind as she was, she was " a very queer lady."

The girl, after doing some shopping on the street, having just been paid a week's wages in advance, and spending some time with other domestics of her acquaintance at the houses where they were employed, reached home after dark. She was the only child of her widowed mother, a lynx-eyed, spectacled dame, who dwelt alone in a little house, save at such times as her daughter was able to be with her.

She greeted her entrance at this time with much surprise.

" What's the matter now, Em ? " she inquired.

" Oh, nothing but another holiday," the girl cheerfully answered. " Mrs. Bashford wants to be alone till morning, and, the Lord knows, I'm willing she should be."

" And it was only yesterday you went back, after a day's holiday," the dame sharply commented. " Look here, Emmy — I don't know about this. I hain't been half satisfied, all along, about it. You get good wages and have easy times; but sometimes I think 'tain't just respectable, all this bein' alone of your missus."

" Well, never mind, mother," said the daughter, lightly. " If Mrs. Bashford can stand it, I guess *I* can."

" Maybe *I* can't, then! " old Mrs. Grove protested. " I'm a respectable woman, and I mean to bring you up respectably, Emily — or Emilia, if that suits you any better. I don't like your having service at a house where you ain't allowed to attend more'n half the time. It don't look respectable. You just go back there, and come in on that big lady kind of sudden, and see what she's up to."

" Mother, I shan't do it! I'm ashamed to have you mention such a thing. Mrs. Bashford has been kind to me, and I won't sneak round in any such way, to spy on her."

" You won't? "

" No."

" Then I will. I've seen enough of this, Em. I don't like it; we've got to have an understanding about it."

The daughter protested; but Mrs. Grove was in earnest, and, putting on her bonnet and shawl, left the house.

She returned in less than half an hour, in a state of great excitement; and the report she made was mingled with sobs.

Mrs. Grove had, at first sight, found the house very dark. She had rung the door-bell, without answer. Trying the door, she had found it locked.

She had passed round the house. All was dark, until she came along the verandah at one side. There a very faint ray of light shot out under the partially-lowered curtain. The blinds were closed on all the windows on that side; at one window she managed to unfasten and open them.

Then she saw what almost caused her to scream with fear!

She saw that the light came from a bed-room, beyond the parlor. The door between was open.

She saw the foot of the bed. She saw a white, delicate hand thrown over the foot-board. She saw a woman's head hanging over the side of the bed, toward the foot, with hair all disheveled and sweeping the floor. Hand, arm, head were motionless.

All this she saw with one horrified glance, and ran screaming from the spot.

She burst in on her daughter, at home, terrified and excited. She managed to tell her what she had seen.

" Well, I declare !" Emilia pettishly exclaimed. "What of it all? If Mrs. Bashford wants to eat canned lobster and have bad dreams, as she often does, why shouldn't she? That's all there is of it."

" No, no!" Mrs. Grove vehemently protested.

" There's horror in that house. I wouldn't step foot in it for uncounted gold. O Heaven, such a sight!"

The girl was not only unconvinced, but angry. She was determined, now, to vindicate her good mistress, and to show that all was in her house as it should be.

Emilia put on her hat and wrap and started. Mrs. Grove, begging her not to go, followed after.

Emilia reached the house, and by aid of her own door-key entered. She did not remain five minutes. She burst out, crying and screaming, and joined her mother far up the street.

" Do you believe me, then?" Mrs. Grove asked.

" O, my God, yes! — 'tis dreadful! Poor Mrs. Bashford! what shall we do?"

" Go for Dr. Eldridge," her mother said.

The girl accepted the advice, and the two started together. It was a long walk to the doctor's; they arrived there, only to be told that he was attending a wedding-party at Mr. Gregory's.

Emilia hastened thither. She arrived after the bridal party had departed, after the unceremonious rush of Ernest Mulford into the house. It was her white, scared face that was thrust into the parlors, calling for Dr. Eldridge.

The doctor accompanied the woman to the house. He went in, they following him fearfully.

He was in the chamber a moment alone. There was pause and silence.

" Come in here! " he said. " You must see, as well as I. You will have to be witnesses."

They entered reluctantly.

The dark hair still swept the floor; the head still hung over the side of the bed.

" Look at the eyes, " said the doctor.

They were fixed and staring, with the pupils strangely dilated.

" Feel of her hands. "

They were stone cold.

"PRUSSIC ACID. THAT'S HER STORY."—Page 154.

" See here! "

He lifted up from the stand an empty vial.

" Smell of it; it will not harm you to smell. "

They did so. It had the bitter odor of crushed peach-kernels.

" Prussic acid, " said Dr. Eldridge, briefly. " That's her story. "

It was not quite all her story. A sealed package was found under the pillow, addressed to Weston May-hew. On the next day, when the news of his death came to Bardwell, the package was opened by the coroner. It contained the unhappy woman's state-ment and confession.

CHAPTER XXXI.

THE VOICE OF DEATH — MRS. BASHFORD'S CONFESSION.

THIS is the 18th day of September, 1877. It is now four o'clock in the afternoon. I am alone here in my house at Bardwell. I have sent my servant home, that I may not be interrupted in my design.

It is no ordinary design. I am proposing to kill myself. I am perfectly ready and willing — *yes*, anx-ious! — to die; but I don't want to be tormented in body on the passage from one world to another. Of course, I couldn't go to Dr. Eldridge, or any other doctor, and ask him which is the easiest form of suicide. So I have had to investigate for myself. I have been for some days reading up on the subject, and I have decided in favor of prussic acid. If you take half an ounce of it, of ordinary strength, you are dead in two minutes.

So *that* question is settled. That shall be my way.

Well — I suppose that to-morrow the doctors and the officers of the law and a lot of gaping men will gather about my poor, cold clay, whisper to each other that this woman was surely mad, to make such an end of herself.

My dear sirs, don't make any such mistake! I am perfectly sane; if I were not, I shouldn't have deliberated so long on the easiest mode of ending it all. I shouldn't have gone to Randolph, two days ago, to get the poison, for fear that it would excite remark if I got it here. Mad! Why, when a woman has nothing to live for, why shouldn't she kill herself? That is what I have often thought; that is what I am going to put in practice now.

I write this to explain myself. I mean it for the only person on earth that I love, and who no longer loves me. If it falls into his hands, he will read it and burn it. That will be well. But should it by chance fall into other hands, then the people of Bardwell will know how I have loved and suffered. These are my last hours; I care not how it be.

I have not dared to address it to *him*, as I shall address the envelope. My love would overcome me. I should seem to be talking to him, right here before me, and I should break down. O Weston, Weston Mayhew! you do not, you never can know how I love you!

There is his name; the name of him who is all the world to me, without whose love this world is empty and hollow.

Good people of Bardwell, should this ever meet your eyes you will wonder to learn that I am his wife. Yes, his lawful wife, wedded to him in far-off California, almost twelve years ago. And you will wonder that it could be so; and good wives and matrons among you will sneer, that I can claim now to be his wife for the first time.

Well, sneer at me, if you will. Only let me say that the kind of love that I have for this man is a kind that you know nothing of. I told him once that I loved him well enough to die for him. It was true; I am going to die for him.

Let me tell this bitter, yet blissful story briefly.   He knows how true it is.

I was a romantic girl, just grown to womanhood.   I was full of passion and impulse, as well as romance. Like most creatures of that kind I had my ideal.   I saw Weston Mayhew, and he realized to me every dream of my life.

I don't know whether he had ever loved, or not. He told me that he had never married; that he had no parents living, no brothers nor sisters, nor children of brothers or sisters; that he had no relatives on earth but two distant cousins.

More than once since those happy days he has reproached me that I courted him.   If it was so I could not help it.

No, I could not help it.   He loved me in a kind of way, I suppose, as all men love all women.   Yes, I will be candid; he warned me that I had better not marry him.   But I did, just because I loved him, and he indifferently consented.

From that day to this I have consented to keep our marriage secret, just because he wished it.   When he left California, giving me ample means to live on, he made me promise that I would not follow him.   That promise I meant to keep.   But our boy, my idol, died. I hungered for this man's love; I braved his displeasure, and made the weary journey here.

Here for two years I have secretly enjoyed the love that he chose to give me.   Nobody has suspected the truth.

But I might have known that this could not long go on.   It is he that has brought on the end.

Very lately he told me with his own lips that he expected to marry that pert creature, young June Gregory.   He laughed at me when I protested, with tears, against such wickedness, and told me that I could enjoy his love just the same; that we could keep everything secret, just as before.

Do not mistake me. I am none too good for that, if I could make up my mind to share him with another. But I can't. He shall be mine alone, or life will hold nothing further for me.

Five o'clock — I put aside my writing, put on my wrapper and slippers, and have walked about the house, viewing all the familiar things that it contains. It is all so pleasant, it is hard to leave it all! Oh, why cannot he find his happiness here with me?

I have learned that he will marry June at half-past eight o'clock to-night. He has tried hard to keep it secret, but after what he told me, I have been suspicious, and have laid a dozen traps for the truth. I have secured it in one of them, no matter how.

O cruel, cruel man! He knows me all too well. He knows that I never could betray him — never could give him over to the law! I love him too well.

Yet he does not know that I love him too well to share his love with another. He will believe it to-morrow!

Six o'clock—I have been sleeping in my chair, I believe. My thoughts went away over the mountains, almost to the Pacific, to the glen where my boy — *his* boy — is buried. Shall I meet dear little West to-morrow. I wonder — if I— if—

Half-past seven—I know I have slept, this time; a glance at the clock tells me so. I have awakened calm and clear in my mind. I am resolved!

Just now I went to the shelves, and looked where I have ever kept our marriage certificate. I wanted to look for the last time on the link that binds us two together — binds us, though he will not own it, nor let me avow it. I had it in mind that I would give it one long, lingering look; that I would kiss it, perhaps; and that then, for his sake, and for the sake of his happiness with his new wife, I would burn it, before I go hence.

It is not there. Some hand has removed it. Whose but *his* could it be?

Well, it is but another pang in the hour of death. Let it go. It has been an empty possession to me. To see it now would not comfort me.

These last lines are written in my chamber. I shall not be disturbed; they will not find what is left of me till morning.

Let me steady myself before I go. Let me take a last thought of this world and its people.

It seems strange, does it not? — that you can pass so quickly from one world to another!

I have said it before; let me say it again, in my dying moment! Life is sweet to me; but I give it up, because it is necessary for *his* happiness that I do so. I die for him. I give him all I have.

O God, pardon me! O Christ, have mercy upon me! This it is, to love too well!

I hear the ticking of the clock; a faint sound of distant laughter and footsteps reaches me. Five minutes hence — what shall I hear — what see?

My work is almost done; a few more words, and I shall lay this weary pen aside. But I shall sign this paper with my rightful name, for the first and last time; with the name *he* gave me.

The vial is before me, with its colorless, deadly draught. Welcome the sudden, quick relief that it brings!

No more — no —— 　　　　　　　PHEBE MAYHEW.

CHAPTER XXXII.

THE DETECTIVE'S NEW REVELATION.

ONE week had passed since the return of June Gregory, her father and lover, to Bardwell. The coroner's jury had viewed the remains of Mrs. Phebe Mayhew, as she must now be called, taken the testimony of the servant, her mother, and Dr. Eldridge, and returned a verdict that the deceased had died from the effects of poison administered by herself. Hardly anything but the strange events that we have been recording was talked about in town, and the press had taken them up and published them far and wide through the land. It may be doubted if any case that, on account of its peculiar circumstances and surroundings, never got into court, ever excited more comment or interest than did the famous " Mayhew case."

We will introduce the reader to the pleasant sitting-room of the Gregory mansion on the Saturday afternoon which closes the week referred to.

It is the pleasant hour after dinner, when a family-circle and its guests may sit and chat in that quiet enjoyment that is found nowhere but in a home. Mr. Gregory and his wife, much subdued by the late terrible experience, and the narrow escape of their little family from disgrace and ruin, were deeply thankful for that escape. Ernest Mulford had informed them of the large share of Mr. Lear in the success of his own efforts, and they had invited the detective to dine at their home on this day. Ernest was there, also; and as June was not yet able to walk about, and hardly strong enough to stand, he claimed the privilege of drawing her in her easy-chair back and forth between the sitting and the dining-room, and to sit by her, that he might attend to her wants.

Mrs. Gregory had recognized in the detective an old friend and acquaintance of her young days at Dinsmore. The subject of the early love of this man for her sister Jane was rather too delicate a one to be much talked about, even in this small circle; but from the little that Mr. Lear permitted to be said upon it, Ernest saw that the tender recollections which Mr. Lear cherished for his deceased mother had prompted him to come so powerfully to his own assistance in this critical time.

The detective was restive under the warm acknowl-
edgments and fervent thanks showered upon him by
the four persons present.   He tried to protest that " it
was all a matter of business," and that " such things
have become easy to me, by long experience;" but it
would not do.

" I want to know how I can reward you, sir,"
Ephraim Gregory warmly said.   " I am not exactly
rich, but I am comfortably well-off.   Money cannot
pay for such service as you have done for us; but anything in reason you can ask me for."

" I shall ask you for nothing, Mr. Gregory, except
to be a guest occasionally in your house, should I
remain in this part of the country, as I am quite likely
to do.   It is as you say; there are some things that
money cannot pay for.   Of that sort is all that I have
done, or may be able to do, for the son of Jane Mulford
— and for the lady whom I hope before long to salute
as Mrs. Mulford," he added, bowing to June, who
smiled, colored, and was not offended.   " Money is no
object to me; otherwise I should not have left the
Great West, where of late the year has been a poor
one that has not yielded me ten thousand dollars in my
vocation.   Now, let us change the subject.   Mr. Mulford will remember that on the evening when he
returned with you and your daughter, Mr. Gregory, to
Bardwell, I told him that there was a most astonishing
revelation to be made, which would be of the greatest
importance to him and Miss Gregory; but I refused to
inform him then what it was, as it seemed better to
wait until I could give it to you four together.   That
time has now come."

They were all attention and listened eagerly while
he proceeded:

" First, I will read you the confession left by that
unhappy woman who was lately buried by the side of
the man she loved with such an absorbing, I might say
such an unreasoning, passion.   Poor creature!   In

death she has received what was wrongfully, basely denied her in life — recognition as the lawful wife of Weston Mayhew. That she was his wife, there cannot be the shadow of a doubt.

" I attended the coroner's inquest that was held over her and directed the attention of the coroner to the importance of securing proof upon one point in that investigation which had not occurred to him; I believe it had not occurred to any person but me. My experience in such cases made me of some assistance upon that inquiry, and when I asked the coroner to allow me to make a copy of Mrs. Phebe Mayhew's dying confession, explaining 'to him the use that I wished to make of it, he cheerfully consented.

" You will much better understand what I am about to tell you by first hearing that confession."

He read it to them. It is unnecessary to say that they were deeply affected by it. There was not a dry eye in the room when he had finished; his own voice trembled a little toward the close.

" Let us now call your attention," he said, " to certain facts that were developed on the inquest.

" The servant-girl, Emilia Grove, testified that her mistress dismissed· her for the day on the afternoon of the 18th, at a few minutes past three.

" Both she and her mother testified that Emilia reached home shortly after seven o'clock.

" The conversation that followed between the two occupied some minutes. It seems that Mrs. Grove had become suspicious about her daughter being sent away so often by her mistress. She thought that there was something wrong in the frequent desire of that lady to have her servant away from the house. Mrs. Grove is a strict woman, of Scotch descent, and very watchful as to anything that could bring reproach upon her daughter. She ordered Emilia to go back and find out what was going on. The girl had a real regard for

A Sharp Night's Work 11

her mistress, and she flatly refused.   Mrs. Grove, with considerable temper, put on her bonnet and shawl, and started herself.

"At this point of the inquiry, I whispered to the coroner, and he asked some minute questions.

" 'Mrs. Grove, can you say what time it was when you left your house?'

" 'Aye, sir, I can.   I looked at the clock, and saw that it was twenty minutes to eight.'

" 'Are you quite certain as to that?'

" 'Certain sure, sir.'

" 'Can you tell how long it took you to go to Mrs. Bashford's house?'

" 'Not more than ten minutes.'

" 'How can you be positive of that?'

" 'Well, sir; in *this* way: More than once within a few weeks past, I have walked straight there from my house, to see Em about something or other; and once I timed myself, just out of idle curiosity, and found that it took just ten minutes.   On the evening of the 18th I was a little provoked by Em's stubbornness, and I know I walked a little faster than usual.'

" 'You swear, then, that you got to Mrs. Bashford's as early as ten minutes before eight?'

" 'That's it, sir; I'm positive of it.'

"The daughter, I may state, thoroughly corroborated her mother as to the question of time.

"I resume my story.

"Immediately upon arriving at Mrs. Bashford's, Mrs. Grove rang the door-bell.   Without waiting to have it answered, she tried the door.   It was locked. The house was dark.   She went along the verandah, and at one of the windows, I presume the same one where I made important discoveries one night, she made the first discovery of the tragedy of *that* night.

"She unfastened the blind, and looked through the window under the curtain.

" What she saw, she described in a few abrupt sen-
tences. I copied them from the coroner's minutes."

The detective read from another slip of paper.

" I saw the bed-room door open. The chamber was
lighted from a lamp that I could not see. I saw the
foot of the bed. There was a hand thrown over the
foot-board. A woman's head hung over the side of
the bed, her hair loose and sweeping the floor. The
face was toward me, turned upside down, and the great
eyes were fixed, and staring in the most horrible way.
She was perfectly still; not a hair of her head moved."

" Upon seeing this terrible sight," the detective went
on, " Mrs. Grove rushed home in a panic. Her daughter was incredulous as to the story that she told her in
a few gasping words, but went immediately back to the
house, her frightened mother following a long way
after. Emelia entered the house by means of the key
to the front door that she had always been allowed to
have, and repaired to the fatal chamber. She found
the body of her mistress in precisely the position that
her mother had described, and perfectly motionless.
The girl was terrified, as a matter of course; but she
testified to two items that are of the greatest importance, and which show that she had her wits about
her.

" One was, that she lifted up Mrs. Bashford's arm,
and that it fell like lead when she let it go.

" The other was, that her eye happened to rest on a
small clock on the chamber-mantel, as she fled from the
room.

" The hands pointed to twenty minutes past eight.

"What followed, you have heard about. The almost
frantic women, in their search for Dr. Eldridge, did
not reach him till more than an hour later, when Emelia
found him in this house, soon after the arrival of Mr.
Mulford. The doctor went immediately to the death-
chamber with the women, reaching there, as he thinks,
shortly before ten o'clock. He found the suicide dead,

the body still remaining in the position in which both the women had seen it. He called them in to take particular notice of its appearance, of the empty vial on the table, strong with the scent of prussic acid, and of the disordered appearance of the bed, plainly showing a dying struggle.

" Right here, remember that the last entry of time in the confession is *half-past seven*, and that there is little written after that.

" Dr. Eldridge's testimony was very direct and positive.

" 'The woman died of prussic acid,' he said. 'A few drops remained in the vial, which I analyzed, and I find it the strongest and deadliest solution of that powerful poison known to the medical science. Much less than half an ounce would kill a healthy person in two minutes.

" 'Judging from her appearance as seen by Mrs. Grove,' the coroner asked, ' do you think she was then dead or alive?'

" 'Dead, unquestionably.

" 'And when seen by Emelia Grove a little later?'

" 'Dead, of course. Her experiment with the arm would show it.'

" 'But you saw the corpse shortly before two, as you say. You then gave it a careful examination. How long, in your judgment, had this woman been dead at that time?'

" 'I can speak with positiveness. It could not have been less than two hours.'

" Now, Mr. Gregory," said the detective, " you may tell us when your daughter was married to Weston Mayhew."

" At precisely half-past eight," was the prompt response. " I timed it with my own watch."

The detective looked at June and Ernest, as they sat together. A shadow of the meaning of these strange developments was stealing over the girl's face, but the

quick mind of Ernest had already leaped forward, and
grasped the disturbing *truth*.   He started up and held
out both hands in entreaty.

" For God's sake, Mr. Lear, say no more! For June's
peace of mind, please drop the subject. You have been
our friend; don't distress us with such a shocking fact
as all this evidence points to. "

" My dear Ernest, I *must* go on!   I must state the
truth, just as it is, just as my close investigations have
established it.   It is not to distress either of you; it
is to lead the way to the most astounding part of this
whole affair, and one that you will both rejoice to
know.

" First, then, it is established by certain proof that
Phebe Mayhew, wife of Weston Mayhew, died before
eight o'clock on the night of September 18th.

" Second, that Weston Mayhew was married to
June Gregory at least half an hour later.

" *Mr. Mayhew, then, had been a widower at least
thirty minutes prior to this last marriage!*

" He no doubt intended to commit bigamy; but he
did not.   Unknown to himself, he was legally free, and
capable of marrying again, at half-past eight.   You,
Miss Gregory, then became his lawful wife.   You are
now his lawful widow.   Your name is Mrs. June
Mayhew. "

CHAPTER XXXIII.

RECOMPENSE.

AT this startling announcement June uttered a low
cry, and placed a hand on Ernest's shoulder, as if fear-
ing that some undefinable harm was yet to come to her
from her dead and buried husband of half-a-day.
Ernest threw an arm about her, and looked anxiously
at the detective.   Mr. and Mrs. Gregory were troubled
and distressed.

Mr. Lear went rapidly on.

" Be assured, my friends, if it had been merely to establish a curious fact, I should never have taken all this trouble.   I had a definite object in view from the first.   I saw consequences of the largest kind depending upon the proof of the fact that I have just stated to you.

" Return now, for an instant, to the deceased Mrs. Mayhew's confession.   Mark her words, where she says of her husband:

" *'He told me that he had no parents living, no brothers nor sisters, nor children of brothers or sisters; that he had no relations on earth but two distant cousins.'*

" After reading that statement, I was very anxious to verify it.   For the last three days I have employed the telegraph across the continent to establish the truth of those words; and I have entirely satisfied myself that they are true.   I learn that the sole surviving relatives of the deceased, Weston Mayhew — excepting his widow — are two persons living in Sacramento, both wealthy, and both cousins, three degrees removed.

" Mr. Mayhew, as you all know, left an estate valued at two hundred thousand dollars.   It consists entirely of personal property; it is all in this State.

" To whom will the law give it?

" The facts, as you have seen, I have settled beyond a question.   Now let me read an extract that I took to-day from the statute-book of this State:

" *'If the deceased leave a widow, and no descendant, parent, brother or sister, nephew or niece, the widow shall be entitled to the whole surplus.'*

" I think you understand me now!   Mrs. Mayhew, I can understand how it may be a very disagreeable thing, after everything that has happened, for you to bear that name; and I think you are quite correct in desiring to change it speedily to some other name — Mulford, for instance.   But I tell you that your right to that name also gives you the right to two hundred thousand dollars, left by the deceased."

There is a certain bewilderment caused by such an announcement as this, that no person is superior to. The detective leaned back in his chair, enjoying the amazement that he had caused. Mrs. Gregory was the first to find her tongue.

" O, June! " she cried. "Ought you to take it? "

The girl looked at her lover, silently appealing to him to answer.

" If you leave it to me to say," said Ernest Mulford, slowly and deliberately, " I am perfectly prepared with an answer. That bad man has gone to his account; it is not for us to judge him; I am not judging him in what I shall say. But just reflect on how the last two months of his life were passed! All that man could do to blast the good name of another he did towards me. He separated June and me by his falsehoods; he kept us separated by his crimes; he sought deliberately to make her the innocent victim of his unhallowed desires, to ruin her happiness for life, as well as mine. And he almost succeeded! Heavens! I shudder now, when I think by what a narrow and desperate chance he failed in condemning June to misery. Well, out of the strange complications of this case it seems that the law gives his property to her. He has two very distant relatives, both rich. Shall June take it? Why should she not? I regard it as some recompense to her for what she has suffered. Not very often does the law deal so justly and righteously as it will with her. Shall she take it? I say *yes*, most assuredly."

" And you are quite right," said Mr. Lear.

CHAPTER XXXIV.

LAST SCENE OF ALL.

WHEN, a few weeks later, Ernest and June became husband and wife, and came into possession of this for- tune, they did not forget those, who by their tireless devotion during those tremendous and critical hours of the night of the 18th and the morning of the 19th of September had helped make their happiness possible.

They took no " wedding-tour." The mere mention of the name caused Mrs. Mulford to shudder, from the associations it recalled. Their honey-moon was passed in the quiet and comfort of the Gregory mansion.

They varied their own happiness, they added to it, by going about and doing good to those who had aided them when they sorely needed help.

Their first care was for the widow and orphan child- ren of the heroic engineer who had died at his post of duty. They visited the widow, they condoled with her, and surprised and delighted her with a check for five thousand dollars.

The fireman, too, was remembered in a substantial and most acceptable way.

Ted Vaun had insisted on being carried to his home near Drayton, as soon as the doctor would permit it. There they found him, in bed with his broken leg, but cheerful, and delighted to see them.

They stayed an hour with him. He highly enjoyed the visit, and expressed no end of gratification that everything had turned out so well. Ernest told him that he should pay all the expense of his sickness, and that he might call on him for anything he wanted.

" Oh, I will — when I want anything," Ted re- plied. " Don't know when that'll be, though. One thing I want, though; when I get able to drive again, I want to take you two on a long ride behind them animals. Nothing like 'em in these parts. But for that cussed stone they'd have have got you through in time, *sure!* David came right back home himself, that night. They're powerful good hosses — but, as I told you, David is a leetle — just *a leetle* — the best."

The kind Bartrams were not forgotten. For some years Wally had fretted under an uncomfortable mortgage on his little place. Ernest paid it off, and he and his wife gratified the honest pair by making them a day's visit.

Emmett Ashley had no need to be helped in a material way; but he was a guest at the wedding, where few were invited, was running over with good nature and was proud in the friendship of the bride and groom. He took a personal interest in happiness that he had done so much to secure.

That wedding was a quiet, unostentatious affair. Through dark ways and devious paths these two had finally reached their happy goal. And " all's well that ends well."

It is the wedding night. The simple ceremony is over; the supper has been eaten; the congratulations spoken, the guests have departed. It is late at night; the house is still and dark.

But not entirely dark. In the chamber of Elias Lear, still an honored guest at this mansion, and urged to prolong his stay, a light burns.

The detective has been sitting alone for an hour. He has been thinking of the past; the recent past, the past far gone. Tenderly, sadly has he thought of it. The happiness of June and Ernest has given him the deepest satisfaction. He thinks of them as though they were his own children. But his thoughts go back to another, whom he may not see. The old man becomes young again. He takes her picture from its place near his heart; he gazes with a kind of rapture at the beautiful face; he kisses it again.

"I have done what would have pleased her," he murmurs. "Does she not know it?"

And he seeks his tranquil pillow, as one who knows that the greatest blessing of this life is:

"To learn the luxury of doing good."

THE END.

MILWAUKEE & NORTHERN R. R.

THE
SHORT ∴ LINE
FROM
CHICAGO (Via C., M. & St. P. Ry.)
—AND—
MILWAUKEE
—TO—
IRON MOUNTAIN and MENOMINEE, MICH.

MARINETTE, WIS.   **FT. HOWARD, WIS.**
GREEN BAY, WIS.   **DE PERE, WIS.**
NEENAH, WIS.   **MENASHA, WIS.**
APPLETON, WIS.

MARQUETTE, Mich.   *HANCOCK, Mich.*
ISHPEMING, Mich.   *HOUGHTON, Mich.*
NEGAUNEE, Mich.   *L'ANSE, Mich.*
REPUBLIC, Mich.   *CHAMPION, Mich.*
CALUMET, Mich.

And all Points on the G. B. W. & St. P. Railway.

PULLMAN PALACE SLEEPING CARS
ON ALL NIGHT TRAINS.

C. F. DUTTON,   **W. B. SHEARDOWN,**
General Superintendent.   General Ticket Agent.

WILWAUKEE, WIS.

KANKAKEE LINE,

THE POPULAR ROUTE BETWEEN

Chicago, Lafayette, Indianapolis & Cincinnati

The Best and Quickest Route between Chicago and Chattanooga,
Atlanta, Macon, Savannah, Jacksonville, Florida,
and all points in the Southeast.

THE ENTIRE TRAINS

run through without change between Chicago, Lafayette, Indianapolis
and Cincinnati. Elegant Parlor Cars on Day Trains. Pullman Sleepers
and Luxurious Reclining Chair Cars on Night Trains. Pullman Sleeper
Cars through without change from Cincinnati to Jacksonville, Florida.

Special Pullman Sleepers between Chicago and Indianapolis. Passengers arriving in Indianapolis at 3:25 a. m. may remain in the car until
8 o'clock. North-bound, the car will be ready to receive passengers at 9 p. m.
and will stand on spur track west of Union Depot.

Trains depart from and arrive at Lake Street, Twenty-second Street
and Thirty-ninth Street Depots, Chicago, the Union Depot, Indianapolis,
and Grand Central Passenger Station, Cincinnati, which is situated in the
very heart of the city and in the immediate vicinity of the principal
hotels and business center.

Connection with all Trains

of Cincinnati Southern Ry., C. W. & B. and C. C. C. & I. Ry., are made
in the same depot at Cincinnati, thus avoiding the tedious omnibus transfer
incident to other lines.

Tickets for sale at the principal ticket offices.

For detailed information, Time Tables, Maps, Rates of Passage of
The Kankakee Line, Address

J. C. TUCKER,

Gen'l N. W. Pass. Agt., 121 Randolph St., Chicago.

JOHN EGAN, Gen'l Pass. and Ticket Agt., Cincinnati, O.

THE GREATEST DETECTIVE STORY
EVER WRITTEN.

This sterling romance possesses all the strength of a marvel-ously developed story of detective experience, and yet has a grand, realistic basis upon which it is founded. ITS OFFICIAL RECOG-NITION IS MADE MANIFEST by the following letter:

City of Chicago, Department of Police,
CHICAGO, August 1, 1886.

GEO. W. OGILVIE, Publisher, Chicago, Ill.:

DEAR SIR—In furnishing the facts concerning the celebrated Artesian Well tragedy, which form the initial chapter of " Manacle and Bracelet," we have given many details hitherto unknown to the public.

The dark deeds committed by the criminal classes are often hid by impenetrable mystery, as in this noted case, and the sagacity of the police, the shrewdness of the assassin, and all the elements of intrigue and plot, present in such tragedies, have been woven into a romance of rare interest, with what is most unusual, a basis of solid facts.   Truly yours,   JOSEPH KIPLEY,
JOHN D. SHEA,
Chiefs of Detectives.

No pains or expense have been spared in the illustrations of this story, and it will delight the reader and open a new and varied field of genuine detective exploit. " Manacle and Bracelet " is no ordinary romance, and will prove beyond doubt the great success of the year.

FOR SALE BY THE NEWS AGENT ON THIS TRAIN.

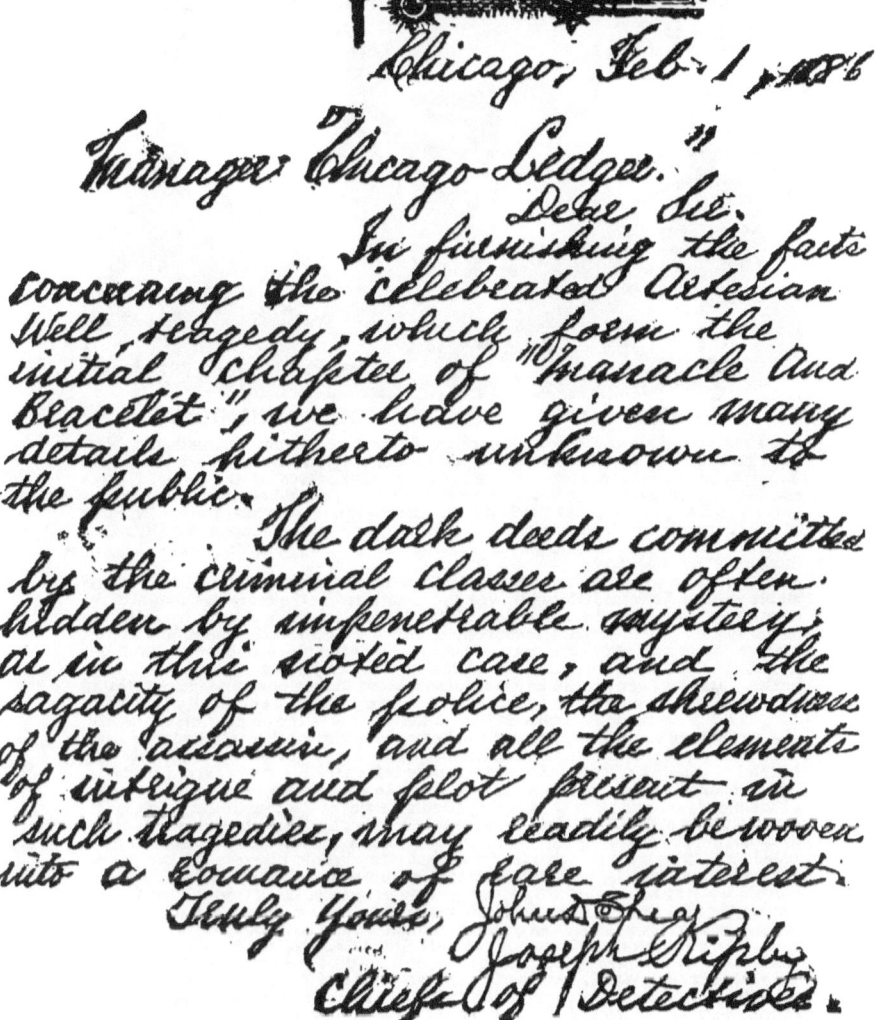

City of Chicago
DEPARTMENT
POLICE

Chicago, Feb. 1, 1886

Manager "Chicago Ledger."
          Dear Sir.
          In furnishing the facts
concerning the celebrated Artesian
Well tragedy, which form the
initial chapter of "Manacle and
Bracelet", we have given many
details hitherto unknown to
the public.
          The dark deeds committed
by the criminal classes are often
hidden by impenetrable mystery,
as in this noted case, and the
sagacity of the police, the shrewdness
of the assassin, and all the elements
of intrigue and plot present in
such tragedies, may readily be woven
into a romance of rare interest.
          Truly Yours, John Shea
                    Joseph Kipley
          Chief of Detectives.

www.ingramcontent.com/pod-product-compliance
Lightning Source LLC
Chambersburg PA
CBHW031113020726
47495CB00007B/2183